Christmas 1995   Whitehorse.

To Isaac

MW00979233

Happy reading adventures.
Love,
From:

Stuart & Mum x x x x

Over to you Charlie and Micah
dose
G'ma Kate +
G'pa Stuart.
x x

WHERE HAVE YOU BEEN, BILLY BOY?

Also by Monica Hughes

WHERE HAVE YOU BEEN, BILLY BOY?

Monica Hughes

HarperCollins*PublishersLtd*

First Edition

Canadian Cataloguing in Publication Data

Hughes, Monica, 1925-
  Where have you been, Billy boy?

ISBN 0-00-224389-X

I. Title.

PS8565.U34W54 1995   jC813'.54   C95-931382-6
PZ7.H84Wh 1995

95 96 97 98 99 ❖ HC 10 9 8 7 6 5 4 3 2 1

Printed and bound in the United States

To the students of Mary Fritsch, Ridgewood, New Jersey, who already know a lot about carousel animals.

CHAPTER ONE: 1908

The boy ran along the street, his bare feet slapping against the pavement, his heart thumping in his chest. He heard an angry shout—Stop, thief!—and ducked into an alley. Here welcome shadows hid him from the gaslight glare of the main thoroughfare. He shrank against the sooty wall, trying to make himself thinner than he already was, thin enough to be invisible.

The cry came again, closer now, the words loud. "Stop, thief!"

Heavy feet pounded past and he plastered himself even closer to the grimy wall.

The shouting and footsteps faded into a welcome silence, broken only by the distant clip-clop of horses' hooves and the occasional racket of an automobile. The boy hunkered down on his haunches, his back against the wall, indifferent to the dirt and the smell of rotting vegetables from the garbage bins and cartons that hid him from those walking along the main street at the end of the alley.

He began to bite into the bread roll he had clutched in his left hand throughout the chase. Just one roll, one lousy roll, not even fresh, and the cops had been after him like a shot. He swallowed the first few chunks quickly but, once the roll was half eaten, he made himself chew the rest slowly, taking the smallest possible bites, making it last as long as possible.

When it was finished he gave a deep sigh and looked up at the small strip of sky that was visible between the walls of the stores that bracketed the alley where he hid. It had been twilight on a hot June evening when he'd snatched the bread from the bakery some blocks away. Now, when he looked up, he could see a few stars in the narrow slit of sky. Soon it would be quite dark.

The dry bread had made him thirsty. He'd have to go looking for water. And he couldn't stay here anyway, not all night. The cops patrolled the alleys after dark, stirring up the old drunks and other homeless men from their sleep with a booted foot in their ribs.

In many of the elegant city squares there were drinking fountains. In the boy's head was a vague map of the city, marked with places to sleep, places where food might be found, like the garbage bins of the fancy hotels, and places to hide, like this alley. But this evening he'd run for blocks with the cops at his heels and lost count of where he'd got to. Somewhere out there he'd better find water, and a place to spend the night where he wouldn't be caught and turned in.

He got stiffly to his feet and began to walk down the alley, not the way he'd come, but towards the street at the other end. Not that he was afraid of the cops, not now, with the evidence of his theft safely in his belly. But the other street just felt luckier.

The pavement was cooler now beneath his hardened bare feet, though he could still feel its grit and summer stickiness. He trotted along steadily, his eyes looking this way and that, alert for any unexpected peril. Block after block, stumbling over the high curbs, dodging the carriages and newfangled automobiles that crowded the busy streets, he hurried on. This was the hour when the streets were full of people going out to dinner and on to the theatre. They weren't part of his world and he hardly regarded them, any more than he stopped to look in the brightly lit windows of the restaurants. The backs of restaurants and hotels, where the garbage was tossed out, were of more interest to him. But right now he could think only of a drink of cool water and a safe place to sleep.

The music began to draw him, like a moth to a candle. It was faint at first, gradually becoming louder as he trotted on, block after block. It had a beat to it—oompa, oompa—drums and whistles and brass. Cheerful music. Music to march to. His tired legs picked up the beat and he jogged towards it. He'd heard music like this somewhere before, at a place with a ferris wheel and a carousel. There'd been an admission fee, probably would be here too, but the idea of that didn't stop him. There were always ways into places like this for those who didn't have the money to pay: cracks in fences, gaps in hedges. He slid like a shadow along the perimeter of the gardens, found a broken railing and slithered through.

Even though it was now almost dark, the carousel was still crowded with children, girls in bunchy gathered skirts with brightly coloured sashes, boys in sailor suits and shiny boots, laughing, waving at their families, from the backs of bright-eyed prancing horses, lions, sea monsters, painted creatures out of a world of dreams. The boy crept close, his thirst forgotten, his eyes greedily taking in the brilliant colours, the glistening gilt trim, the lively eyes of the animals. Oh, to ride on one of those. . .

Slowly the carousel unwound towards the end of its journey, the stirring band music stopped and the riders jumped down or were lifted to the ground and whisked away. The gardens began to empty. From his place in the shadows the boy reached out to touch the brown neck of an Indian pony, its head proudly raised, a carved wooden rose, so real he could almost smell it, tucked into the harness below its ear.

"Hey, you!"

He jumped and ran, dodging between the remaining visitors, and vanished into the shadows. Slowly the gardens emptied. He stood motionless, trembling with fear and fatigue, among the bushes. No one came after him. The lights along the paths were put out one by one. There was a bottle lying on the path close by. He could see that it was still partly full and his hand snaked out and pulled it into the safety of the bushes. He crouched down in the darkness and drank the pop, warm, flat and sticky sweet. After he'd finished he felt thirstier than ever, but he didn't dare leave his hiding place and look for a drinking fountain. There was sure to be a watchman walking the paths, making sure everyone had left before locking the gate.

Steps crunched loudly on the gravel and he ducked down, hiding his pale face and hands from the gleam of the man's kerosene lantern. The night stick, swishing at the bushes that lined the path, caught him a painful blow across the shoulder, but he swallowed his cry and didn't move. Crouching against the damp ground beneath the hedge, he waited, and his waiting turned into sleep.

He woke with the moon shining full on his face. Lucky the watchman hadn't been by, he thought, as he stretched painfully and crept out to look for a safer place to sleep. It was very still. No horses or automobiles. No lights in any of the buildings around the square. Not even a hunting owl. Then he heard it: the faintest creaking sound, a whisper of air over something moving.

His eyes darted to and fro, but he could see no one. Then the moon slid past a cloud and caught a gleam of gold. Just a flash. He might have imagined it. But in a blink it was back again. The boy crept towards it and his mouth fell open. "Jeez!"

The carousel was moving, horse chasing giraffe chasing sea monster, round and round, faster and faster, the creatures riderless, as if they were going on their own for a moonlight gallop to some unimaginable place. He crept closer.

There *was* one rider, astride a great horse, armoured and proud. He glimpsed grey hair and a straggly beard streaming back in the wind, like the tails of the horses. Faster and faster spun the silent carousel, so fast that it seemed that the animals must all spin off into space and hurtle up among the stars.

He was dreaming, the boy told himself. Nothing in the world could move so fast. The man and the animals spun by in a blur. He could feel the wind of their passage lifting the hair on his forehead, see the candy wrappers and ticket stubs fly up in a whirlwind. Now there was nothing but a blur and, beyond it, a strange shimmering. He blinked, knuckled his eyes and opened them as wide as he could. Where'd the carousel go? And the old man?

It was unanswerable. A puzzle, like much of the world out there. He shrugged and slipped away among the shadows, found a water tap with an iron mug attached by a chain, drank deeply, and then curled up under a bush away from the bright moonlight.

His empty belly woke him and, as he rolled over and groaned, a smell drifted into his nostrils. It drew him from his hiding place, shivering and stiff-legged, and led him across the gardens, past the carousel—what was that funny dream about the carousel?—towards a shack close to the main gate. The smell turned into the separate odours of bacon, coffee and baked beans. Saliva filled his mouth and he swallowed. The pain in his belly was like a clenched fist. Slowly he edged towards the open door, his right hand up to protect himself from a sudden blow, his left ready to snatch whatever it could. He was quick and clever, that's how he'd survived alone in the city this long; but he was cold, still half asleep, and not quite quick enough. A bony hand circled his left wrist like steel handcuffs and pulled him into the room.

"Watcha got in mind, pal?" The old man's voice was soft, almost grandfatherly, but, as the boy pulled back, the grip on his wrist tightened.

"Nothin'. A fella can look, can't he? No law 'gainst lookin'."

"If that's all you was reckoning on doing. . ."

"Sure." The boy nodded vigorously. The smell of coffee and bacon was almost overwhelming. He felt sick, and the stuffy room, with its rumpled cot, chair and stove, spun around like the carousel. A hand pushed against his chest and he found himself sitting on the edge of the bed. A tin coffee mug was held under his nose. He reached for it, gulped and choked, his eyes watering, his nose dribbling.

"Tsch!" The old man tutted, took back the hot mug and dipped a crust in it. "Here. Try this."

The morsel slid down his throat. He snatched the bread, dipped, bit and swallowed.

"Take it easy, young fella. Not so fast. It won't run away."

The words "run away" triggered an automatic response. His body twitched. He would have jumped up and ran, but the man's hand was on his shoulder.

"Well now, I wonder what *you've* been up to? Not that it's any of my business. I'm not a man to send a starving dog on its way empty, much less a boy. So don't be in such an all-fired hurry. Take your time."

The boy felt the big hand leave his shoulder and he watched suspiciously as the old man took a tin plate, dolloped a big spoonful of beans on it, added three slices of bacon and handed it to him. "And here's a fork. Don't eat too fast or you'll get sick. Sunday morning," he added casually. "Nobody'll bother us today."

The boy watched him spoon beans into his mouth from out of the pot and eat the bacon with his fingers. He took a steadying breath and dug into his own food without another word.

"More coffee?" the old man asked when both plate and frying pan were empty and polished clean with a bit of bread.

"That's okay." He drained the mug and handed it back, eyeing the distance between the bed and the door. Cautiously he watched the old man refill the mug and sip slowly, his twisted fingers clasped around the chipped enamel.

"Ah, that's better! Nothing like a good breakfast to start the day right. 'Bout time we introduced ourselves, don't you think? My name's Johannes Braun." Bright blue eyes peered at him. "Well, come on, boy. Cat got your tongue?"

"Billy," the boy said at last. "I'm called Billy."

"And a lot of other names, I'd reckon, by the look of you. You got a last name?"

"Not to remember."

"Where's your folks, then?"

Billy shrugged. "My ma died. Pa went off looking for gold. Left me with the landlady. She said there was no more money left, so I pushed off."

"How long ago?"

Billy thought. Days were divided in his mind into unlucky days, when he went hungry, and lucky days when he got something good to eat, like now. Today looked like being real lucky. As for months and years, there was cold weather, and okay weather for sleeping out. "It was snowing," he remembered.

"Nobody tried to put you in a home?"

"One of them orphan places? Not me. I can run faster than the p'lice or the truant officers. I'm fast." He rubbed his wrist, where the gnarled hand of Johannes Braun had encircled it. "Mostly anyway," he added.

The old man smiled. "I'm pretty nippy myself, considering. So what say we shake hands, eh, Billy boy?"

Hesitatingly Billy reached out his hand. Johannes shook it heartily. "Good. Now we're pals."

Pals. Billy felt warm inside, warmer than just the beans and bacon and coffee could account for. For the first time he really looked at the old man's face.

Not that old, really. Tired, kind of worn down, with blue eyes that were clear, not red and rheumy like the drunks he'd met in the back streets of the city. His back was bent and twisted, and his hair and beard straggly but clean.

The hair reminded him. "I seen you last night. Where'd you go?"

"Go?" Johannes ran gnarled fingers through his grey beard. "Why, nowhere, Billy boy. I walk around the gardens a couple of times a night, make sure no one's up to mischief. Hiding in the bushes, maybe. Missed you, though, didn't I?"

"Thought I saw. . .must have been a dream then," Billy muttered.

"Funny things, dreams."

Billy could have sworn there was a twinkle in the old man's eyes when he said that. They sat in silence for a while. The little hut was stuffy, the stove radiating heat in the corner. His stomach was full, he was warm. He felt his eyes close and jerked himself awake. "Guess I should be going. Thanks for the grub."

"What's your hurry? Got plans, have you?"

"Just to keep moving."

"Ahead of the police, is that it? You done something real bad, Billy boy?"

"No, honest I haven't. Just pinched a bit of grub now and then. But I don't want them putting me in no workhouse or orphanage. Nothing like that."

"If you're not running, then what's your hurry? You could think about staying."

Billy shrugged, suddenly wary.

"On the up and up," the old man said quickly. "Thing is, I'm not as spry as I was. It's the rheumatics. Hit my back first. Dare say you've noticed it. That's when I had to quit work. Lucky to get this job. Now, taking tickets and running the carousel, keeping her in good trim, I can handle that just dandy. But running around picking up garbage is a bit more than I can manage, the way my back feels some mornings. With me so far?"

Billy nodded.

"So I reckon if I had a young fella, like it might be you, to be my legs and back, to do the running around and picking up, it'd be worth it to me to offer lodging and grub and some clean overalls and a decent pair of boots. What d'you say?"

"You mean, stay *here*?" Billy looked around the cosy room, with its cot, stove, chair and table, stuffy with the mingled smell of beans, bacon, coffee and general frowziness. No more dirty alleys and hard pavement, no more picking over rotting garbage. "Stay here? With you?"

Johannes flushed. "It's not much. Pretty cramped for your style, I reckon. But it's cosy and out of the rain. I could get hold of an extra mattress. Roll it up and stow it away during the day. Lay it out by the stove at night. What d'you say?"

"I say it's great. Place to stay. Regular grub. Maybe. . .", he hesitated.

"Spit it out, Billy boy."

"Maybe I could say you was my granddad I was looking after. Just if the truant officer or the police come hassling me, you know."

"I reckon that'd be all right." The blue eyes blinked. Then the old man shook himself and went on briskly, "So you can start earning your breakfast right now. This here basket's for the rubbish. There's a bin by the main gate you can put the garbage in, but make sure you save out bottles and anything else looks good to you. I've got a friend gives me good money for those."

"Yes, *sir*!" Billy picked up the basket and hopped briskly along the paths, retrieving bottles and ticket stubs. Easy way to earn a living. Why, he'd got it made! "All done," he reported back.

"Finished already? You're mighty spry, young man. Let's take a stroll around, shall we?" He straightened himself with a grunt, his hand against the door frame.

"You okay?"

"Fine once I'm up. Just getting there's the problem. No, there's nothing wrong with me but years. Come on, Billy boy. And you might as well bring that basket."

"But I've already. . .", Billy protested, running after the old man, who was making good speed down the path.

"Hey, lookee here." Johannes's stick pointed at a candy wrapper caught in the hedge and, a few steps further on, a soft drink bottle rolled among the roots of a bush.

By the time they had strolled down every path that wound through the gardens Billy's basket was full again, and he was beginning to get mad. Who *was* this old guy, bossing him around like he had the right to? Like he was family or something? Maybe it was time to push off after all, Billy thought, kicking a pebble along the path.

He stubbed his bare toe and remembered the old man had promised him new overalls and boots. Real boots that fit. Maybe he'd better stay till he'd got the clothes. *Then* he'd take off. With boots of his own he could do anything, go anywhere. Maybe jump a freight and head out west.

He looked up at Johannes who, even with his twisted spine, was half a head taller than he was. "Thanks for showing me. I'll do good next time, you'll see." He smiled and opened his eyes wide, like he did when he was wheedling a penny out of a passing shopper.

Johannes's blue eyes looked steadily back into his, with a kind of knowingness in them that made him uncomfortable. He ran ahead to dump the trash in the bin near the garden gate.

"That all the work you got to do?" he asked, as he followed the old man back to the little hut.

"Today's Sunday."

"So?"

"Are you a heathen child, Billy boy? Don't you know the Almighty made the Sabbath for rest? Come tomorrow we'll get you overalls and boots. Then you c'n polish up the animals whilst I check the engine."

"Engine?"

"The heart of the carousel, Billy boy. Its beating heart."

Something in the tone of the old man's voice made Billy look at him sharply. It was like Johannes was in love, the way he spoke. With a carousel! But he was old, Billy reminded himself. And old people were crazy, as often as not.

True to his promise, first thing Monday morning, when the bean pot had been cleaned and the frying pan scrubbed around with a bit of old newspaper, Johannes put on a jacket and slipped some coins into his side pocket. Billy had been keeping a sharp lookout, but Johannes was craftier than he'd reckoned, and he couldn't see where he'd taken the money from or how much more the old man had hidden away.

Side by side they walked down the street, turning one corner and then another, plunging into a neighbourhood of narrow streets and mean shops and houses. Johannes stopped by one whose window was so filmed with grime Billy couldn't see inside. He knocked on the door, from which paint hung in curls.

It moved slightly. "We're not open yet," a voice said sharply through the crack.

"It's me, Marthe."

"Johannes, me lovely!" The door swung open and the old man pushed Billy ahead of him into a room crammed from wall to wall and floor to ceiling with tables, chairs and sofas, upon which were balanced piles of secondhand dishes, boxes of cheap jewellery, oil lamps.

"So what you doing here so bright and early?"

"Meet my new pal, Billy boy, Marthe. He doesn't seem to have no last name. Billy, this here is Mrs. Weingarten. She's a friend of mine from the old country."

"Pleased to meet you, Billy." His hand was engulfed in a large moist palm. Mrs. Weingarten was enormous all over, with black shiny stuff swathed over her bosom and pushed out behind in a great bunch of fabric. Her cheeks and forehead glistened with sweat, though the morning was still cool; her hair, piled on top of her head in an untidy bird's nest, was a bright henna red.

She and Johannes began talking in what Billy thought of as foreign moonshine, and he wandered through the shop, fascinated by the extraordinary collection of stuff that filled it. Rusty pans for washing out gold were balanced against tubs and wringer washers, and the dusty tables were covered with vases, statues, lamps and ornaments.

Wonder what I'd get for this? Billy thought, picking up a tiny silver box that fitted neatly into the palm of his hand. Easy to pinch. . .

"Pretty, ain't it?" He jumped as Mrs. Weingarten came up silently behind him and deftly removed the silver box from his fingers. "Called a wafer box. Real silver. Maybe fifty years old or more." She returned it to the desk from which he'd lifted it and, hand on shoulder, guided him across the room to where clothes were piled on chests and shelves. Her fingers bit painfully into his collarbone. Why had he ever thought her soft?

"Here's a pair of overalls looks like they'll fit this fella, Johannes. Good stuff. Feel it. Hardly worn."

The overalls were measured against Billy and laid aside. On them were piled two heavy flannel shirts and two pairs of long johns.

"He won't be needing a coat, not till winter," Johannes said. "But boots now. . ."

"Boots is tricky to fit. Buy 'em big, I say, and a couple of pair of heavy socks. Let the boy grow into them. How about these?"

The boots were tried on and added to the pile of clothes. Billy felt his face hot with excitement. He hadn't had clothes like these since. . .he couldn't remember when.

"And a mattress and a couple of blankets, you said? I've got just the thing." Mrs. Weingarten waddled to the back of the crammed room and showed them a pile of thin mattresses, their ticking stained and torn. "Not a bedbug in the lot, I'll guarantee."

"How can you be sure, Marthe?"

She said something to him in that foreign talk and

they both laughed immoderately. A narrow mattress was pulled from the pile and two blankets, hard and felted with washing, still smelling of yellow soap and mothballs, were added. A discussion over price, more like a fight, followed, ending when Johannes pulled a handful of silver from his pocket, counted out coins into Mrs. Weingarten's fat hand and sealed the bargain by kissing her on both cheeks.

"Can you carry the lot?"

"If you've got a bit of cord the boy here'll roll up the mattress with the blankets. And he can wear his boots. That'll save carrying them."

Billy fought the mattress and blankets into a manageable roll and tied it with a piece of strong cord supplied by Mrs. Weingarten "For free, though I could get two cents for it, easy."

"You're a princess, Marthe." Johannes kissed her again, and they set out, Billy struggling with the rolled mattress, the old man carrying a parcel of overalls, shirts and long johns.

"Here, we're not going the same way home."

"Nope. We'll stop off at the baths and I'll stand you to a good scrub. No point putting clean clothes on a lousy body."

"I ain't. . .", Billy began to protest, but by then they had arrived at the public baths. The mattress was left with the man who took the old man's money and handed out a rough grey towel and a piece of hard yellow soap. Billy was pushed into a cubicle containing a big enamel tub, rust-streaked beneath the taps.

"Fill it good and hot and wash thorough. I'll be back to check behind your ears."

"I'm not a baby."

"So when d'you last have a bath?"

"Don't recall exactly. Not that long."

The old man snorted and left him. The water was blazing hot and Billy shucked off his old clothes and stepped into the water with a gasp. That felt good! He slid down until only his nose was above the surface and lay there basking. He was three parts asleep when Johannes returned, his beard and hair damp and neatly combed.

"Don't look like your body's seen the soap. Sit up and let me have a go at it."

"Hey, that hurts!"

"Gimme the other ear and don't complain. Now your neck."

"Ow, c'mon. You'll have the skin off me."

"When did you last scrub that neck? It's a wonder to me there ain't moss growing on it. This here's the only time I'm acting nursemaid to a kid like you. Next week you'll do your own scrubbing. Let's look at your feet. Now the other one. We'll clip those toenails once we're back home. They're like horses' hooves. Boy, you sure got good callouses under there. How long've you been without shoes?"

"Dunno. Three, four months, I guess. I had a pair in the winter, but someone took 'em off me when I was asleep."

"Well nobody's going to get these ones. Now dunk under and get the soap out of your hair. Let's take a look. Well, you ain't got lice and that's a surprise. Stand up."

Billy stood up and then yelled as Johannes poured a bucket of cool water over him. "Gee, that's freezing!"

"It'll close your pores. Now dry off and get yourself dressed. Might as well throw out that old stuff of yours. Ain't no good for nothing, even rags."

In his new overalls and boots Billy walked beside Johannes, the mattress bundled in his arms. He felt as if he'd lost a skin, the breeze touching his cheeks and neck in a strange tickly way. Kinda nice, but strange too. And they'd be having a bath every *week*, the old man had said. He wasn't too sure he liked the idea of that.

By the time they had reached the gardens, Billy's shoulders were aching from the awkward bulk of the mattress, and he had blisters on both feet. He dropped the bundle, undid the laces and eased his feet out of the boots.

Johannes hammered two nails into the frame of the hut. "You can hang your spare clothes on these. And your boots too, when you're not wearing them. Guess you'll have to break them in slow like. But I bet in a week you won't want to be without them."

CHAPTER TWO: 1908

"Watcha doing, Johannes?" Billy leant against the painted boards that hid the drive mechanism from the rest of the carousel.

"What are *you* doing is the question, ain't it?"

"I'm through, honest. I've polished the brass and cleaned the leathers and scraped the gum off the animals. Gee, those kids are dirty, leaving their gum all over the horses' bellies."

"You'd never do a thing like that, of course." Johannes looked up from his work with a twinkle in his blue eyes.

"Course not. They're lovely. Can I help with the engine?"

"Just about finished." Johannes wiped his hands on an oily rag and straightened up with a groan.

"What's that handle there?"

"That's the clutch mechanism. Connected with the

gears down here. Start slow, you see, and then speed up once the platform's moving. Takes a while. It's a weighty thing."

"And what's that?" Billy pointed.

"That's the governor. Makes sure we don't go too fast."

"What'd happen if we did?"

Johannes laughed. "It'd spin us off into tomorrow, Billy boy!"

In a sudden flash Billy remembered something that had completely gone out of his head in the last two days. Waking up under the hedge with the moonlight on his face, hearing the whisper of the carousel moving faster and faster, seeing the old man on the lead horse, his hair blowing in the wind. Faster and faster. Until they vanished.

He remembered too that he'd asked the old man about it the next day and been put off with a laugh. Just a dream, Johannes had said. But was it? He peered closely at the mechanism that Johannes had called the "governor". It seemed to him that the rod could move forward way past the place where it was supposed to go, and further back, too. And there were marks on the metal casing surrounding the slot through which it went, faint scratch marks. He rubbed his finger over them and found his hand batted back.

"Don't you *ever* touch that!" The old man was blazing, his eyes snapping fire, his cheeks suddenly red.

"I didn't mean. . .I just wondered. . ."

"Wondering'll get you nothing but mischief. Work's what you need. If there's nothing left to do you can run and pick up a bite for our supper from Mr. Cassidy."

And that was all Johannes would say. Later, jogging along the street with a parcel of ends of stewing beef, Billy couldn't help wondering about what he had seen that moonlit night. And he decided that he'd stay awake and see if the old man snuck out at night to go riding the carousel. Or if it had just been a dream, like he'd said.

For the next two nights Billy tried to stay awake, but each night, wrapped in a warm blanket, lying on a clean dry mattress, his eyes closed and his healthy, well-fed body slept. And when he opened his eyes again, it was always morning.

On the third night he again fell asleep before the old man, but was wakened suddenly, perhaps by the moon, which was shining in through the little window directly into his eyes. Sleepily he turned on his side, watching the silver path of the moonlight from window to door. A shadow broke the line of light and, now fully awake, Billy saw Johannes get out of bed, pull on his overalls over the long johns in which he slept, and slip silently out the door.

His heart beating like a hammer, Billy forced himself to lie still, to give the old man time to reach the carousel. Then he too slipped out of bed and, without bothering to put anything on, went out into the moonlit garden. The bushes and trees were still. Not a leaf trembled. The moon, a few nights past full, cast a silver spell over everything, and Billy followed its silver path towards the carousel.

He moved quietly from bush to bush until he was close enough to see the carousel clearly. It was just beginning to move. Forgetting all caution he ran forward, intent on climbing aboard too, but by the time he was close enough to the platform, it was already moving too fast. He saw the giraffe, a green snake wound round its elegant neck, stretching high above the other animals. He saw the glint in the lion's eye, its open-mouthed roar. The dappled grey leader spun past and then his favourite, the Indian pony with the rose tucked in its harness. The giraffe again. And again. Now they were only a blur. A shimmer made his head suddenly hurt, so that he had to shut his eyes for a second or two.

When he opened them again the carousel was slowing down. The giraffe shot past pursued by the lion and the pony. Now it went by more slowly. He realised suddenly that in a few minutes he'd be caught out, spying on Johannes. He ran down the path to the shack and dived under his blanket.

How loud his breathing was! How hard his heart was beating! He shut his eyes tight, pretending to be sound asleep. Behind him he could hear steps crunch on the gravel, the squeak of the door opening and then closing. The soft slither of cloth as Johannes shucked off his overalls. The squeak of the bed frame. Then silence.

What'd happen if you did go too fast? His own question echoed through Billy's head. And then the old man's answer. *You'd spin off into tomorrow, Billy boy.*

Was *that* where Johannes went when the shimmer came?

And what did *tomorrow* look like?

With these unanswerable questions tumbling around in his head, Billy finally fell asleep.

He awoke to sunshine and the comforting smell of coffee brewing on the stove. As if nothing extraordinary had happened.

This is tomorrow, Billy puzzled out in his head, as he lay, still half asleep, watching the old man potter around. And it's just like yesterday, ain't it? Yesterday. Today. Tomorrow. They're all just different ways of looking at NOW, ain't they? So where does the old man really *go*?

He came back to these unanswerable questions over and over again through the rest of the day. He'd find himself standing, polishing rag in hand, wondering.

"Well, spit it out," Johannes said abruptly in the middle of a silent midday dinner.

"What?" Billy looked up from his food, startled. "Nothing wrong with this grub."

"I mean, why don't you tell me what's been bugging you all morning."

Billy felt a guilty flush creep slowly up his neck and cheeks and settle into the tips of his burning ears. *He'll be mad if he finds out I've been spying on him. Might throw me out. I'll never find another cushy place like this, not in a million years.*

He managed a weak laugh. "Ain't nothing pertikler. Just something you said the other day."

"So?"

" 'Bout the carousel. Like if it went too fast it'd spin you off into tomorrow."

A funny look came into Johannes's eyes. It was a look Billy was familiar with. He'd seen it in the eyes of a lot of people he'd rubbed shoulders with during the year and a half he'd been on his own. In the eyes of people on the run, people with secrets. A kind of guarded defensive look. Only Johannes wasn't a *criminal.* He couldn't be.

Billy watched the old man with a puzzled frown as he carefully scraped the frypan clean, and went on scraping, long after it was clean enough.

"I said that, did I?" The old man spoke at last.

"You sure did."

"So what's your problem?"

Billy tried to put into words his thoughts about "tomorrow" just being the place you got to after "today" was over, the place separated by a sleep. "Only suppose you don't go to sleep," he went on. "When does 'today' turn into 'tomorrow'? What's the real difference?"

"Hmm." Johannes tugged his beard. "That's what you might call a deep phi-lo-soph-ical question. Why, there's men in universities spend their whole life arguing about those kinds of questions."

"They *do*?" For a moment Billy felt a warm glow inside at having thought up such an important question. Then he realised that the old man had side-tracked him, that he was no further ahead. What he *really* wanted to know was where Johannes actually *went* and what it was like behind the shimmer. At that moment, on a fine afternoon, Billy first got the idea of riding the carousel himself.

It was an idea that got bigger and bigger over the next few weeks, kind of like a weed sprouting up in the flower bed, small and green and of no account at first; but, before you knew it, it had grown into something like bindweed, shooting up inch by inch until it was big enough to wrap itself around the nearest flower, squeezing it tighter and tighter in its struggle to reach the sun.

Billy found himself hurrying through his daily chores, skimping on polishing the brass and rubbing up the leather harnesses, just so he could watch Johannes work on his beloved engine.

"What are these marks for?"

"Where. I don't see no marks."

"Right here." Billy pointed to the plate that covered the gear box.

He looked into the old man's face and saw in it a longing to deny what was in front of Billy's eyes.

Johannes ducked his head and got busy oiling something he'd just oiled a second ago. He couldn't lie, Billy knew. He was good clear through. Not like others Billy'd known.

He waited, his heart beating hard; but when the answer came, it didn't answer his questions.

"Don't pry into what don't concern you, Billy boy."

"But. . .", he burst out. "That first night, remember? I *saw* you ride the carousel. I saw what happened. And it wasn't a dream. I *know* it wasn't."

"So, what *did* you see?"

"It went faster and faster. Then all shimmery like."

"Hmm. You seen that happen since?"

Billy swallowed. "I guess so. 'Bout five nights later."

Johannes snorted. "Spying after me."

"No! Not *spying*. Honest. Just. . .curious."

"Anyone ever tell you what become of the cat?"

Billy nodded, his cheeks hot. Curiosity had killed it, hadn't it? It was a fair warning. He said nothing more and Johannes went on working as if nothing had happened.

But he hadn't answered Billy's questions. Just put him off. Inside Billy a grudge began to grow. He nursed it along. Helped it grow bigger.

They were supposed to be friends, weren't they? Him and the old man.

Sure, he owed a lot to Johannes: a warm safe place to sleep; three square meals a day; his clothes and a hot bath regular every week.

But he'd done a lot in return, hadn't he? He'd worked hard. Helped the old man out. Done as he was bid. Didn't the old man trust him? That's what it came down to. How could they be real friends, even like grandpa and grandson? Not without trust they couldn't.

These thoughts went round and round in Billy's head, making him more and more bitter, until he was ready to quit. Only he'd need a grub stake to set off on his own. And he'd never found out where Johannes kept his money. Whenever they had to buy groceries or pay for their weekly hot bath, the old man always managed it so that Billy was elsewhere when he got out his silver. It was hid somewhere in the shack, but where? Billy had looked under the mattress, but it wasn't there.

Four weeks after they first met Johannes got sick. Whatever it was that had crippled his hands and twisted his back got another grip on him. "I can't budge," the old man groaned.

"What about the machinery? D'you want me to oil it like you do?"

"No. Don't you lay a finger on anything."

Even on his back and in pain, the old man was peppery, Billy thought, as he ran off. Once by the carousel, he couldn't resist another look at the engine. He put one hand on the gear shift, the other on the governor. Then he mounted the Indian pony and tried to imagine what it'd be like to spin off into tomorrow.

It was late afternoon when he got back to the shack, and Johannes was much worse. His face was as grey as cement, and sweat trickled down his forehead.

"Who's going to run her tonight?"

"It's a Sunday, remember? I'll be better tomorrow. Got to be or I'll lose my job. This place. *Everything.*" His gnarled swollen hands clutched the top of the blanket.

When he said "everything" Billy knew, as if he could read the old man's mind, that he was thinking of the carousel—not the wonderful menagerie animals with their shining glass eyes and their tails of real horsehair, but the engine and where its power could take him.

"Got to get help." Johannes struggled up on one elbow. "Look there, in the corner behind my bed, Billy boy. There's a loose board. Found it? My cash box is hid under there."

Billy's heart pounded as he pried up the loose board with his fingernails. Sure enough, in the dank cobwebby darkness underneath was an oblong metal box, not very big, about six inches by four by four. He lifted it out of the hole, brushed it off with his sleeve and set it on the old man's lap. It felt real heavy. So *this* was Johannes's stash!

He watched him take a key, hung on a string around his skinny neck, unlock the box and lift the lid. He edged close, to see how much the old man had stashed away, but his hunched shoulder blocked the view.

"Here." Johannes dropped a couple of coins into his hand. "Go to Mrs. Weingarten. Tell her I'm took bad again. She'll know what to give you. Put the box back before you go. You can't trust people these days."

Billy set off down the sunny deserted streets. In the distance church bells were ringing for evening service. All the rich people sitting in their pews, dressed in fine silks and top hats and all, and probably thinking about their Sunday dinners cooking back home. He looked at the coins in his hands. *A whole dollar!* How much more was stashed in the metal box under the floor? Going to waste. The old man'd never need it all. Would he even miss it?

Mrs. Weingarten's door was closed and locked. He

banged on it with his closed fist. When there was no answer he kicked at the door with his boots. Finally he heard shuffling feet and a faint voice.

"I'm closed. What's wrong with you? Can't you leave a body in peace on a Sunday evening?"

"It's Billy, Mrs. Weingarten. Johannes is took sick."

He heard the bolts being drawn back, a key slowly turned in the heavy lock. The door swung open. "Come in, boy. So what's the trouble with the poor old man?"

Billy described what seemed to ail Johannes.

Mrs. Weingarten nodded. "His old trouble." She sighed heavily. "Ach, the poor man. A great carver he was, before the rheumatics took hold of him. You'd never know it, to see him now, would you? No more'n a caretaker, him that used to carve them beautiful animals."

The dapple grey, the giraffe, the roan. . . Had Johannes once carved *them*? Wordlessly Billy held out the coins, hot from the tight clasp of his hand.

She shook her head and clicked her tongue. "Silly old fool. He wants me to sell him a bottle of brandy to kill the pain. It'll do that, I guess. Maybe kill him too. What he needs is a doctor, but they won't come out for the likes of him and me. And he won't go to the hospital. Can't say I blame him."

Billy shivered. From what he'd heard on the streets, hospital was where you went when it was all up, and you only came out feet first and into the graveyard. "So what'll you do? He's real sick."

She sighed heavily. "Oh, I'll sell him the brandy. I've got no cure for what ails him. At least the brandy'll ease his pain, and if it helps him die quicker, I dare say he won't complain either. You wait here and don't touch nothing."

She vanished behind a heavy velvet curtain that screened off the back premises, leaving Billy alone in the front room. He looked around at the clutter of old furniture. There were the little silver boxes he'd seen before. But she'd probably counted them before she left, he reckoned, and was certainly capable of holding him down and going through his pockets if he tried to lift a couple of them. So he stood in the middle of the room, shuffling his feet, until she reappeared with a dark dusty bottle in one hand.

"You can tell him that maybe it ain't Napoleon brandy, but it's a sight better than the rot-gut they sell in the taverns. At least Johannes has got the sense not to poison himself with that hooch. I'd better wrap this up for you, or you'll have nosy folks interfering, what with it being a Sunday and you under age."

She wrapped the bottle in a piece of checkered cloth and put it in a willow basket. Then she looked at it, head on one side, like an enormous bird. She waddled away and presently came back with a long loaf of bread and a jar. "Home baked. See if you can get the old man to take some of it, with a little soup. Good chicken broth I made meself." She put the loaf and jar on top of the wrapped bottle, and the basket suddenly became an innocent collection of food that a lad might be carrying to his sick grandpa on a Sunday evening.

"Don't drop it, that's all! And let me know how he is when you bring the basket back. Off you go, then." She pushed him out of the house, and he could hear the bolts being shot across before he'd walked down the steps.

When he got back he found the old man half sitting, half lying, in what seemed to Billy to be a horribly uncomfortable position. His face was grey and his

eyes were partly closed, but they opened and brightened when he saw the bottle. "Thank the good Lord
for Marthe! Will you open it, boy? There's a
corkscrew with the kitchen things."

Billy struggled with the cork and finally got it out.
He poured the brandy into a mug and held it up to
the old man's lips. He sucked it down greedily, choked
and drank again, and a little colour came to his lips.
He lay back on his lumpy pillow, his eyes shut. After a
while Billy could see his twisted shoulders relax as if
the spasm was moving off.

He dozed, drank another mugful and dozed again.
Billy heated the chicken broth and tried to persuade
Johannes to drink some of it, with the fresh bread
dunked in it. The old man ate a small amount, drank
more brandy and drifted into sleep. Billy polished off
the rest of the soup and bread himself. With his
stomach comfortably full he lay on his mattress and
slept.

He woke from a muddled dream in which he was
running through thick mud with Johannes's cashbox
under his arm, pursued by savage dogs that barked at
his heels. He woke to a babble of talk in some
unknown tongue and abruptly sat up, thinking that
someone had sneaked into the cabin and was making
off with the old man's money. Then he realised that it
was Johannes talking, babbling away in some foreign
lingo. He crawled out of bed and tripped, falling over
the brandy bottle that had fallen and rolled across the
floor. He picked it up and shook it. It was empty.

Johannes was sitting up in bed, his cheeks flushed,
his eyes glittering in the twilight. When Billy put a
hand on the old man's arm it was hot to the touch,
like he was on fire. But the muscle spasm that had
knotted him up was gone.

"Lie down again and I'll cover you up," Billy suggested. "Ain't good to catch a chill when you're fevered." The old man ignored his suggestion, but his hand shot out and grabbed Billy's arm.

"Is it time to start the carousel? Who's selling the tickets? Never missed a day since she was set up here. Keep her in perfect trim, I do. She'll go for a hundred years. Yes sir! No complaints, never."

Billy was about to tell him that it was a Sunday, that there'd be no rides to worry about tonight, but he shut his mouth again as the old man went on. "You'll have to run her, Billy boy, if I'm not able. Can you do it?"

"Sure I can. Seen you do it hundreds of times, ain't I? Nothing to it. Sell the tickets. All aboard. Make sure everyone's seated proper. Then start her up and slip her into low gear nice and slow. Then change up. And up into top gear and away we go."

"Ten times around. You can count to ten, can't you?"

"I know. Then slow down. No jerking. Everyone off. Then take the tickets for the next ride."

"Good boy. Good boy." Johannes let Billy lower him onto his lumpy pillow and cover him to the throat with the blanket. Then he started up again, clutching Billy's wrist. His hand was fiery hot, like the brandy had set fire to his sickness and was burning it out of his body. "It's the governor you've got to watch. That's what the man said that made the engine. He did something crazy to it. Lost his job because of it. But a man's gotta reach out for his dream, ain't he? Grab the brass ring, huh? Get that extra ride free."

Billy held Johannes firmly, as the old man threshed about while the fever raced like wildfire through his brain. Billy felt hot too, and his heart was racing. Maybe at last he was going to hear the truth.

"The governor?" he prompted.

"When it's off there ain't no limit I can see. I tried it three times. I dunno where I went, but I saw 'mazing things. Automobiles like you'd never imagine. Machines flying in the sky. Buildings higher than the mountains! Wonderful. Another world, Billy boy. Like you never seen before."

"I wanna see it, Johannes. Let me. Please."

The grip on his wrist was astonishingly powerful, like a band of iron. Billy tried to pull his hand away. "You're not to go. Never. It's *my* carousel. Mine. Don't you touch that governor." He began babbling in that foreign lingo again, at first loudly, then in a mumbling voice. Finally his grip on Billy's wrist relaxed and he fell back on his pillow and began to snore heavily.

Billy peered at him anxiously. The old man's face was calm, the pain all smoothed away. Billy tucked the blanket securely across his chest, his arms neatly laid by his sides, and then sat on his own mattress to think.

It's another world, Billy, like you never seen.

Don't touch the governor.

The old man snored softly, his breathing regular. Outside it was dark and silent. The moon was rising, lighting the path to the carousel. It drew him to the door like a silver cord.

My chance. Maybe the only chance I'll get.

He slipped outside, dressed only in his long johns. His bare feet were silent on the gravel path. The trees hung heavily down towards the bushes. It was all black and white. No colour anywhere. The moon had risen above the trees, a white lopsided face, one cheek slightly swollen as if it had the toothache. Ahead of him the triple circle of wooden animals slumbered.

He reached the carousel and climbed onto the platform, his arm encircling the giraffe. From this vantage point he could see almost the whole garden. The shack close to the gate. All was silent.

It's now or never. Just a little spin. I'll be back before you know I've gone, he promised the sleeping Johannes. Slowly he unwound his arm from the giraffe and walked across the platform, through the three magic circles of animals to the centre, to the greatest magic of all, the engine that lay hidden behind the painted panels.

He started up the engine. The racket seemed enormous, enough to waken the dead. Startled, he listened through its clatter, but nothing outside seemed disturbed. He remembered, then, that *he* had heard nothing but a faint whisper of sound when he'd been hidden among the bushes, watching Johannes ride the carousel.

Boldly he pushed the lever into first gear. He felt the tremor as the carousel came to life and the platform began to turn. He felt the animals waken into life. Second gear. Third. Then he flipped the governor aside and pushed the gear shift as far forward as it would go. The platform gathered speed and he made his way quickly back between the animals to his favourite mount, the Indian pony.

The carousel spun faster. His feet automatically found the stirrups. His hands gathered up the reins. He leaned forward against the pony's neck, against the painted rose that hung beneath the harness.

The bushes, paths, trees and flower beds became a green blur. The blur changed colour, growing lighter and lighter until he felt that he was riding through a white mist. He no longer felt that he was spinning round and round. It was more like riding *forward* into the future, galloping into a brilliant whiteness.

He was no longer aware of the giraffe out there

ahead of him, of the lion roaring in his rear. He and the pony were alone in the moon whiteness. It was hard to breathe. He felt frightened, but it was a good kind of fear, like he'd sometimes felt running from the cops, a fear that made him faster, more agile, his brain quicker.

He felt more alive than he'd ever felt in his life before, even while the terror of the unknown gripped him. Was this what Johannes had felt? Was it this feeling that had drawn the old man out night after night, despite the pain of his twisted back? To mount his favourite horse and ride on and on, swifter than the wind.

> *What'll happen if you go too fast?*
> *It'll spin you off into tomorrow.*
> *What does tomorrow look like?*
> *Another world, Billy boy, like you never seen before. . .*

The carousel trembled. The trembling became a shaking. Like it was coming apart. Too fast. Got to slow her down. Billy managed to loosen his hands from their grip on the reins, to kick his bare feet free of the stirrups. He slid down on the right side of the pony, clinging to its saddle for support. Somehow he had to get to the still centre of the spinning. Slow her down before she broke apart.

There was a final mighty shudder. The whiteness was gone and Billy felt himself flying through the air into the darkening shadows. Something hit his head with a shattering blow. Then darkness was all around him.

CHAPTER THREE: 1993

Susan cantered along the fence that separated the north end of their property from the Weltys'. She galloped to get the crossness out of her system, though it was really too hot to ride fast. At the northeast corner she stopped and leaned forward to stroke the sweating neck of her roan mare.

"Sorry, Judy. I'm a selfish pig, taking it out on you."

Judy shook her head, but whether it was to reprove her rider or to deny the accusation of selfishness wasn't clear. Susan laughed, loosened the tie of her cream felt hat and pulled it off. The air felt good and she shook her long blonde hair back and mopped her sweating face and neck with her kerchief, before plopping the hat back on her head.

This was her top favourite place, a rise in the land that gave her the long view eastward into the corn country of Kansas. To north and south small creeks snaked across the flat land, while, to the west, the land lifted, like a tilted platter, to meet the reddening evening sky. Thunderheads were beginning to pile up there, like reflections of the Rocky Mountains that lay, far out of sight, behind them.

Now she'd stopped riding the flies buzzed irritatingly around her face and settled on Judy's sweaty neck. She flapped them away with her kerchief. "I bet there'll be a storm tonight, Judy. Maybe it'll cool things down."

As she watched, the billowy tops of the thunderheads flattened into wide anvil shapes. In a couple of hours there'd be a doozer of a storm. She'd better start back.

As she caught up the reins, ready to turn Judy and walk her westward along the northern boundary of their property, something stopped her. The wind had just got up, flattening the tops of the grain in watery patterns, but it wasn't the wind. Something else close by. A kind of shimmer, like midday heat on the highway, as if the air had been suddenly displaced by something else. And a thump.

Judy flinched, and when Susan soothed her she could feel her neck muscles twitch. "Hey!" She slid to the ground and went to the mare's head. "What's all this about? You're really spooked, aren't you?" Judy stamped a hoof, snorted and showed the whites of her eyes.

"Wonder what that was? Almost like something dropping from the sky." She looked up. The sky was a wide empty blue. No contrails scribbled across it. Not even a hovering hawk. The fence ran in a ruler-straight line to the horizon. Except for the dip where a distant creek lay, there was nothing to see but the round barn that housed Zeke's Folly. Could the sound possibly have come from there?

She hitched Judy to a fence post, lifted the wire and slid between the strands to the other side. The barn used to be on their land, but some complicated dispute that had begun some sixty years before still hadn't been settled. It meant that, though the barn belonged to the Pattersons, the land it was on seemed to be Welty land.

Which was why the two families didn't talk.

She walked through the tall grass, grasshoppers jumping dizzily against the front of her jeans, flopping back with clicks and whirs, a background sound as much a part of life as the prairie dogs and the hawks.

She pulled the barn door open, tugging it over the grass and weeds that had grown up around the threshold. It must have been years since anyone had been inside. As she peered at the shadowy shapes, a rat bolted from a bale of hay. She shuddered and stamped at it with her riding boot as it shot out the door.

"Hello?"

What had she actually seen and heard? A shimmer. A distant thump. Maybe just one of the fighter jets from the air base over to the west.

"Anyone there?"

In her imagination the shadow shapes pricked up their ears and listened. She'd loved this barn when she was a little kid, but now she was almost fourteen years old it felt different. Spooky. Dangerous.

She was about to push the door shut when she heard a groan. A *human* groan. She gave a yelp, told herself not to be stupid, and walked bravely into the darkness.

"Who's there? What's wrong?"

The groan came again, over to her left. She moved

cautiously around the wall, her hand outstretched to guide herself. Her foot touched something soft and she gasped, her heart thumping furiously. Right at her feet a man lay crumpled, as if he were dead. No, too small for a man. A boy.

As she stared down, not sure whether to stay or ride back to the ranch house for help, the figure moved and propped itself up on one elbow.

"Ow, me head!" A young voice, coarse, uneducated sounding.

"What's happened to you? How did you get in the barn?"

He didn't seem to hear her. She turned to follow his staring eyes. Behind her the open door framed the golden fields that reached to the blue horizon. The wide sky.

"Where'm I? Where'd I go?"

"You're in the old barn next to our farm."

"A farm? Nah, I was in the city." He stared up at her. "You a cow hand?" he asked uncertainly.

Susan laughed and pulled off her hat to mop her face. It was as hot as an oven in the barn. "My name's Susan Patterson. This is my dad's place."

"You're a *girl*." He was staring at her jeans and plaid shirt. "But you're wearing *pants*."

"Jeans. Say, where in the world have you come from?"

The boy sat upright, put his hand to his head and said slowly, "*When* is more like it."

"What *do* you mean?"

His face was as pale as his clothes, a loose one-piece outfit remarkably like the old-fashioned underwear that Grandpa still wore in the winter. "Look, Miss, will you tell me something? Honest now."

"Sure."

"What's the date?"

At the absurd question Susan stared and laughed uncertainly. "You've got a bang on the head and you're worried about the *date*?" She looked at her watch. "Well, if it'll make you feel better it's Monday the fifth of July. Okay?"

"But what *year*, Miss? What year?"

"Nineteen ninety-three, of course."

"Oh, jeez!" The boy collapsed onto the dirt floor again. "Nearly a hundred years!"

"Since when?"

"Since last night. In the gardens. It's daytime now, ain't it? I got to get back." He scrambled to his feet and swayed. Susan grabbed his arm.

"Take it easy. You must have had an awful bang on the head. I'd better take you up to the house. My dad'll drive you to the hospital."

"*Hospital?* Not me. Johannes told me about *them*. Come out feet first as likely as not."

"But you need to get your head x-rayed."

"X-ray? What's that? Sounds creepy to me." He shivered.

"You're joking, aren't you?" Susan stared at his pale face and wide scared eyes. "No, you're not joking. Well, at least come up to the house and let Mom look at your head. I can put you up on Judy. She's quiet as a lamb and it's not far."

"Judy's your horse?"

"Yup. She's a roan, a real doll."

"My favourite's an Indian pony, a roan Johannes says it is." The boy spoke shyly, his face getting a little pink. "With a rose under the harness."

Susan frowned. A rose? He really was out of it. She tugged at his arm, but he pulled away. "Don't make me."

"Well, if you won't come to the house, maybe I'd better get Dad to come down."

"No. Don't tell nobody 'bout me. Please, Miss."

"You're in trouble, aren't you? Have you done something against the law?"

He shook his head and winced. "No, honest. I been in no trouble since I been living with Johannes. It's not that. It's. . . I've got to go back, you see? Don't tell no one."

"Okay." Susan didn't understand a word of what the boy was talking about, but it was an adventure, something that was all her own, with no one interfering, like big brother Jim, taking over and bossing, so it wasn't hers any more.

"Look, I've got to get back home for supper. If I'm late they'll start worrying. Afterwards, as soon as I can get away with no one noticing, I'll be back. Food and drink. Some decent clothes. You can't go wandering around like *that*. Promise you won't budge? I'll be back as soon as I can make it."

He nodded, his eyes dazed, as if he wasn't quite taking it in.

"I'll close the door behind me. I hope you won't mind being in the dark. But someone going down the road might notice and get curious." She whisked out and mounted Judy, her thoughts in a whirl.

Alone, Billy sat in the dark, nursing his sore head. It ached and throbbed, and when he touched the top of his skull he could feel a lump like an egg. But his head wasn't the worst of it. He'd done it, hadn't he? He'd spun off, not into tomorrow but into—what year had that strange girl in men's pants said? Nineteen ninety-three. Take away nineteen oh-eight. He tried it on his fingers, but gave up. He'd never been much good at adding and subtracting.

He staggered to his feet. There was a crack in the wooden wall of the barn, big enough to squint through. The light outside was brilliant, brighter than the sunniest day he'd ever seen, and there seemed to be almost nothing but sky. What land he could see was flat as a plate and went on for ever without a single house to break the line of it.

Where were the gardens with their neat flower beds and graveled walks? The familiar smoky air? The little hut where Johannes was sleeping right now, sick and maybe needing him? Above all, where was the carousel that would take him safely back to the familiar places?

A sudden noise, like someone tearing a sheet across, ripped through the sky above his head. He ducked. Something small and silvery shot across the blue, leaving behind it a thin ruler-straight line of white cloud. Not a bird, nothing like.

"I gotta get out of here. I gotta get back home!" He beat at the door and began to cry. How was he going to get there? And who was going to look after Johannes now he was gone?

He was crazy, wasn't he? All that talk about 1908. But she'd look out for him. As Susan rode along the northern fence she tried to concentrate on down-to-earth things, like getting hold of a couple of blankets. That was easy—there were spares in the drawer under her bed. A pair of her jeans would have to do for the boy; he was far too short and scrawny to wear any of Jim's togs. One of her tee-shirts and a pair of socks and runners, if they'd fit—she hadn't noticed the size of his feet. If they didn't she'd be sure to find something in the Goodwill box in the basement.

She decided she'd better take a couple of water bottles and whatever food she could scrounge without Mom noticing. And a flashlight. Too bad there was no electricity down in the old barn.

She checked the list on her fingers. "Don't think I've forgotten anything," she said out loud. "The real problem's going to be smuggling it out of the house without big brother noticing. That storm's going to be a nuisance. I can't take Judy out in the middle of a thunderstorm."

The big dinner bell sounded up at the house. "Come on, old girl. Get a move on. Time for your oats."

She hurried to unharness Judy, rub her down and see to her feed. By then Mom was calling from the kitchen.

"Just got to wash my hands, Mom." She pulled off her boots and ran to the bathroom.

"Oh, phew!" Jim greeted her as she dropped into the chair opposite him at the dinner table. "Been playing in the stables again?"

"Jim's right, Susie, dear." Her mother passed the potatoes and carrots up the table. "You should try to leave time to shower and change for dinner."

"Dinner?" Grandpa, sitting next to Jim, decided to get into the act. "Used to call it supper in my day. What's all this talk about 'dinner'. You'll be serving us quiche and—what's that fishy stuff?—sushi next."

"Don't be silly, Dad," Mom said mildly. "Here's the gravy."

"You know I like butter on my potatoes. Pass the butter, Susan."

"Don't you do it, Susie. Dad, you know it's bad for your cholesterol."

"We all got on just fine before they invented cholesterol. Tell me how come. . ."

The argument washed over Susan as she sat, cut-
ting up her meat, eating her potatoes and carrots
without tasting them. Where had the strange boy
really come from? Obviously not 1908. But there was
no one missing from the county or thereabouts. She'd
have heard on the radio, which Mom kept going in
the kitchen all day. And all that talk, like he really
didn't know what *year* it was. Crazy looking too in
those weird clothes. But she'd find out. He was *her*
secret. That's what was important.

The wind suddenly shook the house, stirring the
pictures on the walls and making the mats creep
along the floor, as if they had a secret life of their
own. The screen door banged and a lounge chair on
the porch fell over. It got darker and Mom switched
on the light over the dinner table.

"Looks as if it'll be a corker. Sure hope there's no
hail up there," Dad said.

"Big anvils," Susan said through a mouthful of
potatoes. "Saw them forming way back over the
Rockies."

"You can't see the Rockies from here, stupid," Jim
put in.

"But I know they're there, don't I, smartie?"

"Children, stop squabbling. Susan, don't talk with
your mouth full."

"Anvils are a bad sign. We sure don't need hail this
close to harvest time. Good dinner, Mom." As Dad got
up from the table, Jim left just behind him. Grandpa
fumbled for his stick and limped into the living room.

"Makes me so mad," Susan muttered.

"What does, dear?"

"Aren't women supposed to be liberated and all

that? But guess who does the cleaning up every day? Us, that's who."

"Come now, dear, it's not so bad. It's only dishes."

"It isn't just the dishes. It's everything. Oh, you just don't understand!" Susan stamped out to the kitchen with a trayful of plates and silverware.

As they dried and put away the last pots and pans there was a sudden flash and a crack of thunder, and the rain began to come down in earnest. Susan peered out the kitchen window. "Darn! Looks like it's set in."

"You weren't planning to go anywhere tonight, were you?"

"Not specially. Just an evening ride." The boy would be wondering where she'd got to. If she didn't get back to him soon he might take off and then she'd never find out what it was all about.

"Challenge you to cribbage," Grandpa shouted from the living room.

"Okay, Grandpa." Susan turned away from the teeming rain. By the time she'd got to the living room Grandpa already had the cards out and the peg board Jim had made for him last Christmas. As they played, Susan's mind was in the barn. Would the boy be frightened of the dark? And he'd got nothing to eat or drink, and it was getting downright chilly now with all this rain.

Grandpa skunked her in the first game. He chuckled. "You're going to have to count sharper than that. You missed fourteen points."

"You should have told me, Grandpa."

The old man chuckled. "All's fair in love and cribbage. Count your own points, Susie-poosie, and I'll count mine."

"Grandpa, don't *call* me that. I'm thirteen years *old*. Almost fourteen. Please."

"Okay. If you give me another game and pay attention this time. It's no fun beating you when your mind's miles away."

The second game was closer. It was ten o'clock and pitch dark outside by the time they'd finished. "Give us a hand up, there's a good girl." His hand grasping his cane, Grandpa stomped off to his room.

"Want a glass of milk?" Mom called from the kitchen.

"No thanks. I'm off to bed." She got into her pajamas, brushed her teeth, and said goodnight to everyone. The rain had stopped and from her bedroom window she could see a few stars. Once the moon was well up it'd be light enough to ride. If only the others would just go to bed too.

While she waited, she smoothed out two blankets on the floor and piled on them a pair of jeans, a shirt, and a jean jacket that she'd tossed on one side till Mom could mend the tear in the cuff. She added socks to the pile and a pair of runners a little bit too roomy for her. She went to the door and opened it a crack. The lights were off at last, just the glow of the night light outside the bathroom lighting up the passage.

She tiptoed along to the kitchen, opened the fridge and stuffed into a grocery bag a loaf of sliced bread, a package of sliced meat, a hunk of cheese, a carton of milk and some apples. The water bottles were in the tack room and she could fill them at the tap there. There should be a big flashlight hanging on the tack-room wall. She remembered a knife to cut the cheese and tiptoed back down the passage to her room. She bundled everything in the blankets, tied them securely and dropped the bundle onto the grass outside her window.

The house was so quiet that she could hear the tick of the clock down the hall. Susan dropped out the window and lowered it behind her until it was open just a couple of inches. In the tack room she filled the canteens and lifted down Judy's harness and saddle. "Sshh, it's only me," she whispered, as she went into the stable. It smelled sweet and warm with horses' breath. Judy was in the end stall, looking a bit dazed, but she stepped obediently out and mouthed the bit as Susan harnessed her.

"Poor girl, did I wake you up?" Had Judy been dreaming? she wondered. Do horses dream? She smoothed the blanket, heaved the saddle onto the mare's broad back and cinched the girth-strap tight. The bundle lay handily across the front of the saddle, drooping down on each side of Judy's neck. The two canteens of water she slung around her own neck, and the big flashlight she hung at her waist.

The moon was well up over Kansas, just the occasional cloud scudding across in front of it, and she could see the trail that led north to the boundary fence. If she took it slowly there'd be no danger of Judy tripping or catching her foot in a hole. Falling like Grandpa.

Dad'll kill me if he finds out I'm riding at night, she thought guiltily. And I wouldn't, except it's life and death. The thought of riding on a life-and-death mission, like a nurse looking for wounded on the battlefield, or, better still, a spy crossing enemy lines, buoyed her up as Judy picked her way deliberately along the trail, flinching as the moon threw shadows across the path, as if she'd never seen a shadow before.

"Oh, come on, Judy, you don't have to be that slow!" But Judy just shook her head and plodded on at her own pace until Susan could have screamed.

By the time they finally reached the barn and she'd hitched the mare to a fence post and hauled down the blanket roll, the moon was almost overhead, a brilliant lop-sided circle that looked like it was cut out of white tin. She pushed open the barn door. "Hi, are you there?"

Silence.

What an idiot she'd look if he'd gone, if there was nobody to be rescued by her rescue mission. But he *can't* have gone, she thought frantically. Not in bare feet and long underwear like Grandpa wore in mid-winter. He'd not get far.

She dropped the blanket roll and the canteens on the ground and unhitched the big flashlight from her waist. The beam caught him, lying in a crumpled heap between two bales. For a horrible moment she thought he might be dead, but then she saw his chest move. She went closer. His dirty face was streaked with tears and he looked very young and helpless, and not more than about ten years old. She hung the light on a nail in the barn wall and gently shook him awake.

"I'm sorry it's so late. I had to wait till the storm was over and everyone was asleep."

He looked up at her blankly for a few seconds and then rolled away, so his face was hidden in the hay bale. "I thought it was a bad dream," he said huskily. "But it ain't. You're *real*."

"Course I'm real. Why ever not?"

"I thought I'd be home in the shack, all snug, with Johannes snoring away 'cross the room. But it ain't like that. I've really come someplace else, ain't I?"

Susan frowned. That bump on the head had really sent him out of it. "Look, try not to worry about that just now. I've brought you some clothes. I hope they fit. And something to eat. Just cold stuff, I'm afraid. Can't risk a fire in the barn."

She was laying out the food on top of one of the hay bales, the plastic bag a kind of tablecloth underneath, when he interrupted.

"Here, these pants ain't got no buttons!"

"Buttons? Of course not. There's a zipper."

"A. . .zipper? What's that when it's home?"

"You're joking, aren't you?" Susan stared. "You mean you've really never seen a zip fastener?" She showed him how it worked, and he zipped it up and down a couple of times and chuckled.

"Where on earth have you come from then, that you've never. . .?"

"I told you. The amusement park in the city. With Johannes."

He choked on the final words and she said hurriedly, "Don't worry. It'll be all right. Have something to eat."

He grabbed at the bread and stuffed half a slice in his mouth; but Susan had to show him how to open the package of sliced meat. He wolfed down half the pack and a hunk of cheese, but he wouldn't touch the milk.

"That's for babbies," he said contemptuously. "Johannes and me, we drink coffee." But when Susan gave him one of the canteens he drank thirstily. Some colour was coming back into his cheeks and he didn't look so panicky. Whatever awful thing had happened to him, the ordinary acts of eating and drinking were making him more comfortable and at home.

"I told you I was Susan Patterson. So what's your name?"

"Billy," he said with his mouth full.

"Billy what?"

"Just Billy. Johannes calls me Billy boy."

"But you've got to have a last name. Everyone does."

He shook his head. "Dunno what it is then. Me mom died when I was little. Me dad looked after me till the gold fever took him bad and he up and left."

"Gold fever? Is that some kind of disease?"

Billy laughed. "You ain't never heard of gold fever? The year of the Klondike Gold Rush, Mom was expecting me. Dad woulda gone then, but she wouldn't let him. He used to talk about it—how, if she'd let him go we'd all be millionaires, with a big house and a carriage and horses."

"Hey, wait a minute. We did a unit on gold rushes in school last year. The Klondike one started in. . .in 1896."

"That'd be right. I was born the next year. I reckon I'm eleven years old and it's nineteen oh-eight right now."

"But it *isn't*. I told you. It's nineteen ninety-three. You *can't* have been born then. You'd be ninety-six."

Billy laughed. "I'm sure not that. Look at me. You're just joshing about what year it is, ain't you?"

"Tomorrow I'll show you the newspaper."

His face went pale again. "I guess I really did it then. What the old man said."

"What?"

"I rode the carousel too fast and got spun off into tomorrow. I guess this *is* tomorrow."

"You rode the carousel?" Susan looked at him blankly.

"In the amusement park. Johannes looks after the engine and that and I polish up the animals, the brasses and leathers and all. I'm real good at it." His face tightened. "I got to go back. Johannes is sick. I can't leave him alone. I got to ride the carousel back, if I can just find it."

"*This* carousel?" Susan lifted the flashlight from its nail and shone it on the centre of the barn.

For the first time Billy saw clearly the vague shapes he'd glimpsed when the door had opened in daylight. He gave a piercing scream, jumped onto the platform, put his arm on the neck of the Indian pony. "What's happened to them all? What've you done? Why are they all broken down and mucky? Look at them leathers! That paint!"

"It's been like this for years and years, Billy, since long before I was born. . ."

But he wasn't listening. He ran across the platform to the centre, where the boards lay cracked, askew, some missing. "Bring the light here, Miss. I can't see proper."

She followed him across the platform and shone the light on the rusty dirt-clogged engine.

He was on his knees, scraping away at the dirt with his fingernails. "It's broke, ain't it? It'll never go. And how'm I going to get home *now*?"

CHAPTER FOUR

Nineteen hundred and eight? It was crazy. It had to be. But on the other hand he didn't know how a zip fastener worked or how to open a sealed plastic package of meat. He didn't recognize a flashlight and he was surprised at her wearing pants. Slowly the truth sank in.

"You really are from. . .from back in nineteen hundred and eight?"

He nodded. "An' how'm I going to get back? Johannes'll be counting on me. He's sick. And. . ." His eyes flashed frantically around the barn. "I don't like it here. I wanna go back." He sniffed.

"Look, please don't cry. I'll help you."

"Crying? I'm not crying. I'm not a babby." Billy blew his nose with his fingers, casually wiping his hand on the leg of his jeans.

She gulped and dug in her pocket. "Here, take a tissue."

"What's this for?"

"To blow your nose with."

Billy obligingly honked into the tissue. "Not good for much, is it?" He dropped it on the floor. "Did you mean what you said about helping me?"

"Of course I did. We'll get this thing going again somehow." She looked doubtfully at the ancient carousel. "I suppose the first thing is to find out what fuel runs it. Like, is it gas or diesel?"

"Coal, I guess."

"*Coal*? You mean it's a steam engine? Oh, well, I guess I can find out how it works."

"But you're a *girl*. Girls don't understand about stuff like that."

Susan laughed. "Things have changed in the last eighty-five years, Billy. Women are surgeons and lawyers and airplane pilots."

"What's that?"

Susan explained what airplanes were and, more vaguely, what actually kept them up in the air. "Though Jim could explain better than me. He wants to be an engineer, if Dad'll let him go to school. But Dad wants him to run the farm. Anyway, I've got to go now. I hope you sleep well. I'll tie the rest of your food up in the plastic bag and hang it up so the rats don't get it." She unhooked the flashlight and hesitated. "Will you be all right in the dark?"

"Course I will." He looked very small standing by the old carousel, her old jeans rolled up at the ankles.

"Okay, then." She switched off the lamp and went out. "I'll leave the door ajar if you like. There's a moon. You can close it in the morning."

"I'd sooner you shut it now. I don't fancy all that emptiness out there."

As Susan rode homeward she tried to imagine what

it'd be like arriving in a strange place a long way in the future. Would this spread still be here in eighty years? Or would the state be covered with big cities and wall-to-wall concrete highways and overpasses? It was a spooky thought.

The moon was high overhead by the time Judy was safely back in her stall, the harness and saddle hanging in the tack room, and the flashlight in its place on the wall. She walked quietly up to the house through the wet grass, the stars trembling overhead. It was so quiet that the noise her window made as she pushed it up sounded shockingly loud. She skinned out of her clothes and slid into bed. In the peaceful space just before falling asleep she thought how awful it must be to have to sleep in a barn, to lie in the darkness of an alien world, with *rats*. She'd have to think up something better for Billy.

She woke with the sun in her eyes and automatically rolled over and buried her face in her pillow. Then she remembered yesterday and sat up with a jolt. She had Billy to look after. Let's hope Mom doesn't have any major plans like making jelly or clearing out the basement, she thought, as she showered and dressed in shorts and a tee-shirt. If so, I'll just have to think up some good excuse. She was first into the kitchen and began whipping up a batch of pancakes.

"Wow, look at you! Turning into a perfect little housewife, aren't you?" Jim lounged in the door.

"Hush up, you. . .you stinker," Susan snapped back automatically, wondering whether she could smuggle some pancakes down to Billy while they were still warm. But what about butter and syrup? Pancakes were nothing without them.

"So what's on your mind, dreamy?"

"Huh? Oh, nothing much." Only worrying how to get a steam engine working. She'd messed about with farm machinery all her life, but how on earth did a 1908 steam engine work? Too bad she couldn't get Jim to help. But if she started asking questions out of the blue, he'd get suspicious, and then he'd never give up till he found out all about Billy. And Billy was *her* secret.

"Susan, how nice of you to make breakfast!" Mom bustled into the kitchen. "I'm late getting started today. Something woke me in the middle of the night and darned if I could get back to sleep again, not for the longest time."

Susan almost apologized and then caught herself. She was supposed to have slept right through the night. What noise? She hadn't heard a noise. She hastily poured another batch of batter into the pan.

"Think Grandpa will want any?"

"Make some for him anyway, why don't you? The boys can always eat them cold for lunch if he doesn't fancy them. I'd better see if he's up. I have to drive him into the city for his eye check-up this morning. I guess we'll stay for lunch and do some shopping. Want to come, Susan?"

Susan's heart jumped. It was an answer to prayer. "No thanks, Mom. I'd sooner ride fences with Judy."

"Not today," Dad put in, passing over his plate for more pancakes. "Jim and I'll need her. We'll be fixing the fences in the southeast corner."

Jim didn't look too pleased, while, on any other day, Susan would have got mad at not being asked to help, but not today. It was working out perfectly. With Mom and Grandpa in the city and Dad and Jim out of the way, she'd be free.

"Better come with Grandpa and me, dear."

"No, really, Mom. There's lots to do here. I. . .I think I'll clean out my room," she improvised wildly.

"Whatever's got into you, little sister?"

"Maybe I just want to have the place to myself once in a while, okay? Dad, shall I fix sandwiches from yesterday's beef? Then you and Jim won't need to come back for lunch."

"Thanks, pet. When'll you be home, Veronica?"

"About four o'clock, I guess, Tom. If I get late you could start dinner, Susan. Better get some steaks out of the freezer."

"Yes, Mom." Susan dished out the rest of the pancakes and poured syrup lavishly over hers, trying to hide the excitement bubbling up inside her.

"It couldn't be better," she told Billy later. "We're totally on our own, so you can come up to the house and have a hot shower. Then I'll get you some decent underwear and cook you a hot meal. You'd like that wouldn't you?"

"You bet."

"We'll have to walk up. Dad needs Judy today."

"Who's she?"

"My mare. Well, she's not really mine, only when Dad doesn't need her. I told you about her last night, remember? Roan, like your favourite."

"You can really ride a horse?"

Susan sighed. Yet another guy who thought she belonged in the kitchen. "C'mon. Let's get going."

As they approached he stared at the sprawling house with the porch wrapped around three sides of it. "Ain't nobody living out here 'cept your family? Ain't you scared?"

"Goodness, no. I love this place more than anything in the whole world. I don't ever want to leave it.

Come on." She led the way into the house. "Here's the bathroom. Clean towels. Soap. Shampoo." She turned away, but then she had to go back and show him how the shower worked and the toilet flushed.

While he was getting cleaned up she ransacked Jim's bureau for undershorts. Then she defrosted a steak in the microwave and set it to fry with some tomatoes and hashed potatoes.

When Billy came into the kitchen he looked different, clean and really quite normal, though his haircut was kind of funny. She dished up his breakfast and sat on the edge of the table, watching him eat.

"I've been thinking. It's going to take quite a time to get that carousel going. You can't stay in the barn. There's no water. There's rats. And sooner or later someone's going to notice you. I think you should stay here with us."

His mouth fell open. "You can't tell them about me."

"Of course not. They'd never believe it. Or, if they did, the newspapers'd find out and the government, and they'd just take you over. And they'd probably put the carousel in the Smithsonian as the only living example of a time machine. No, I've got a much better idea. I've been reading a book about refugee kids in the Second World War. . ."

"What war? Only war I've heard tell of's the Spanish-American war. I remember my dad telling me about that."

"This was a whole lot later. Anyway, these kids were hiding from the Nazis and some people helped them by giving them false identities. That's what we're going to do with you. I've got lots of cousins, some of them in California, some back east. You can be one of them!"

"That's loco. I can't pretend to be your cousin!"

"Sure you can. We'll work out the details now, and then tomorrow you arrive to stay with us. You'd rather live up here than in the barn, wouldn't you?"

"I don't wanna live here nor there. I wanna go *home*."

Susan sighed. "If you're staying here, then you and me will have all day to work on the carousel. I think you'd better be a bit younger. I've got a cousin about ten years old."

"I'm not a little kid. I'm eleven."

"I know. But you *are* small, by nowadays standards, anyway. If you're a bit younger, people won't be surprised if you don't know about things, like World War Two, for instance. And Jim'll leave you alone."

"Who's Jim?"

"My older brother. He's sixteen and he's a real pain. And nosy. But if you're young, I'll be the person told to look after you."

"I dunno."

"It'll work. I promise. D'you want anything more to eat?"

He shook his head. "I'm stuffed. Never ate that much meat before."

Susan rinsed his plate and scrubbed the frypan. It would never do for Mom to ask who she'd been frying steaks for. There was such a lot to remember and so many possible pitfalls. First off was to decide who Billy should impersonate. She pulled out the big photo album from its shelf in the living room and began looking through it. Here were the cousins from back east, Aunt Marian's kids.

"Perfect! Look here, Billy. Here's Bobbie. He was born in 1983 just four years after me. His kid sisters are Alicia and Melissa. Alicia's five and Mel's just three, so there's not much to say about them. Just remember their names, that's all. Bobbie's mom is my dad's sister, my aunt Marian. Her husband is David Stevens and he's a dentist in New Hampshire. Got that?"

Billy nodded. "That kid don't look a lot like me, though. How do they make them pictures such pretty colours? Are they painted?"

"No, that's the way photographs are nowadays. And don't worry about not looking like Bobbie. That picture was taken ages ago, and Bobbie'll be bound to have changed."

"If I'm supposed to be coming from the east to stay, didn't I ought to have a bed roll and some clothes? Even hoboes I seen on the trains got something."

Susan smacked her forehead with the flat of her hand. "Brilliant! I should have thought of that. Let's go down to the basement and see what we can find." She switched on the light and clattered down the stairs.

"Mom keeps a box of clothes for Goodwill over here." She began to pull the stuff out. "Here's some shorts Jim must have grown out of. They don't look too bad. And a couple more pairs of my old jeans. Some tee-shirts. Now we'd better find something to put them in. This case'll have to do. It's kinda battered, but I don't suppose Mom will notice. We'll pack the clothes in it and take it down to the barn. Whoops, I nearly forgot!"

"What's up?"

"You need a toothbrush. And pajamas."

"Nothing wrong with me long johns."

"No, Billy. They *have* to go. In fact I must remember to take them and hide them down in the barn. I think I threw out a pair of polo pajamas last winter.

Kinda like Star Trek uniform, you know. No, of
course you don't. They're a bit too warm for summer,
but they'll have to do. Then they won't be surprised
you don't have a bathrobe."

"Miss—I mean Susan—this ain't going to work. I
don't understand more'n about half what you're saying."

"It'll be okay. Just act shy, that's all. Keep quiet and
watch what I do. It'll be fantastic."

"It's just a game to you, ain't it?" Billy pulled the
case out of her hand and dumped it on the floor.

Susan stared back. "Course not." Then she felt herself turning red. "Well, maybe a bit. It's exciting having a time traveller arrive out of the past. But I *do*
mean to help you, honestly."

"Time traveller? Me? I guess that's so." Susan saw
how Billy looked round the basement, staring at the
workroom with its electric saws, planes and grouters,
each neatly in its place; at the washer and drier; the
exercise equipment Jim had got last Christmas.
"Yeah, I guess that's what I am—a time traveller." His
face was pinched and white.

Susan propped open the door of the barn, so that the
sunlight fell across the carousel. Billy dropped the
suitcase and moved, as if in a dream, across to the
animals. He rubbed the nose of the leader. "Terrible
state this is in. Almost all the paint's gone. This
should be silvery, see, like the horse is in armour.
Wish I could fix them up."

"That's what my great-grandfather planned to do
when he bought the carousel. He put it in the barn
and planned to turn it into a major attraction. But
then he ran out of money when times were bad.
There was a quarrel with the Weltys too. They're our

neighbours. George Welty's in my grade. He's a real pain. Now everyone calls it 'Zeke's Folly'."

Billy wasn't listening. "I guess it'd take a heap of money to fix it up, wouldn't it? Even just the drive mechanism."

Susan had been thinking the same thing and wondering how far the money she'd got saved in the bank would go. "Let's get started anyway. See what it looks like."

When she shone the trouble light onto the machinery in the middle of the carousel, behind the painted panels, she almost gave up. Besides the actual engine there was a mass of pipes, a boiler, a firebox, all rusty and cobweb encrusted. It was evident that rats and mice had made their homes there too.

"There's the main drive what pushes the platform round." Billy pointed. "It looks all right, don't it?"

"I guess so. Well, we'd better brush all this garbage out of the way. There's an old broom over there."

"I'll get it, Miss."

"Billy, you've got to stop calling me 'Miss'. I'm Susan and you're 'Bobbie', remember? We'd better start practising now."

He grabbed the worn broom and began tackling the rats' nests. Something rustled under the platform and Susan pulled her legs out of the way. "I've got to think of how to let Mom know you're coming, Bobbie. Maybe a phone message from Aunt Marian. That should do it. And it'll say you're arriving on tomorrow's bus."

"How'm I to do that?"

"Well, you won't really, of course. Before noon tomorrow morning, you've got to walk south along the road till you come to a big gate. You can't miss it.

There's an arch above it that's got our name on it: Patterson. You can read, can't you?"

"Course I can. Some anyway," he added doubtfully. "Patterson starts with a P, don't it?"

"Hmm. I can see that could be a problem later. Oh well, we'll just have to keep you away from books and stuff. Anyway, you just sit by the roadside till the bus goes by. That'll be about twelve, twelve-fifteen. Once it's gone, pick up your case and walk up the trail to the house."

"Susan, what'm I going to *say*?"

"Don't worry about it. I'll be there to meet you. Just remember that my mom and dad are 'Uncle Tom' and 'Aunt Veronica'. My brother's Jim. And they'll call *your* parents Marian and David. And your little sisters are Alicia and Melissa. Got that?"

Billy nodded dumbly and they worked together cleaning the garbage from around the boiler until Susan glanced at her watch. "Goodness, it's late. I'd better get back home and get cleaned up. I've got that phone message to work out. Will you be all right on your own?"

"I guess so."

"There's lots of food. And don't worry. One way or another I'll help you fix the carousel and get back where you belong."

Though her voice was full of confidence, Susan wondered, as she walked back to the house, exactly how they'd manage it. The machinery didn't look like anything she'd seen around the farm. She sighed and turned her attention to the problem of wording the message from Aunt Marian, so Mom wouldn't phone New Hampshire to find out just why Bobbie had been sent to stay with them. By the time she'd reached the house she'd got her ideas straight and, after a few false starts and crumpled pieces of paper in the wastebasket, she produced a satisfactory message:

> Dear Mom. Aunt Marian phoned. She and Uncle David and the girls are visiting some Stevens relatives, but Bobbie doesn't want to go. She asked if she could send him to stay with us for a month. I said that'd be fine. He'll be arriving on the bus tomorrow. Susan.

Excellent, she thought. Not too many explanations to cause trouble later. And writing it out like that made it seem more like a story and less like lying to Mom. She really hated the idea of that. Already she hadn't been exactly straight, taking food, not that Mom'd grudge that, not to mention the Goodwill stuff, though Billy was certainly every bit as deserving as the people for whom the clothes were eventually intended.

She put the message by the phone in the living room. It was all in a good cause, after all. I bet the people who hid those children from the Nazis had to lie some, she told herself. Then she decided to clean her room, just in case Mom wondered what she'd been doing all day. Cleaning helped ease her conscience a bit and passed the time too. She was surprised when she heard the station wagon bumping up the trail from the road. The car door slammed. The screen squeaked.

"Anyone home? Susan, are you there?"

"Hi, Mom. Hi, Grandpa. There's an important phone message for you, Mom," she shouted from her room. Somehow not looking at Mom made this bit easier.

There was a pause. Grandpa shuffled down the passage and went into the bathroom. She straightened the horse figurines on her dressing table. "Susan!"

"Yes, Mom." She went into the living room. Mom was standing with the note in her hand.

"This is most extraordinary. Is this all Marian said?"

"That's it." Susan managed a casual shrug.

"But if he's arriving on the bus tomorrow he must have left home before she phoned."

Bother, thought Susan. *I blew that one.*

"Or perhaps they were already on the road. Did she say where she was phoning from? Which member of David's family?"

"Uh-uh. Mom, where's he going to sleep?"

"Oh, dear, let me think. Bobbie'd be nine or ten by now, wouldn't he? He'd better bunk down with Jim."

"Oh, no!" That'll be fatal, Susan thought. Jim'll start asking him questions. No way Billy could fool him. "Can't he sleep in my room? There's lots of space now I've cleaned up."

"Nonsense, dear. What *would* people think?"

"He's only a little kid."

"And you're a young lady. There's a folding cot down in the basement. Jim and Dad can haul it up when they get back. I hope Jim's room's tidy."

"Mine is." Susan tried again. "And Jim'll *hate* having to share with a little kid."

Her mother looked at her, her head on one side. "Since when did you worry about your brother's feelings? And cleaning out your room when I hadn't even asked? Hmm. I wonder if you're sickening for something." She pretended to feel Susan's forehead.

"Oh, *Mom*! I guess I meant that B—Bobbie'd hate it. With him being ten and Jim sixteen."

"Most ten-year-olds hero worship their older cousins. It's not like being a brother. Not the same tensions."

Susan sighed. *Darn it, Mom's probably right*, she thought. *Billy—I mean Bobbie—will think Jim's the tops. He'll want to make friends and then he'll start blabbing. And it'll all come out.*

And where will I be. On the outside again, that's where.

She tried to shake the mean thought from her head and went into the kitchen to help Mom with the dinner.

Jim was surprisingly agreeable to the news that he'd have to share his room. "Bobbie? I think I remember him from that time we went east when I was about eleven. Bright little kid. I taught him checkers and he caught on real well. I wonder if he still plays."

Great! thought Susan, slumping in her chair at the dinner table. *How come I don't remember that? Oh, well, I'm committed now. "Bobbie" and I will just have to bluff it out.*

She worried right through the dishes and three games of cribbage with Grandpa. When she finally got to sleep after tossing and turning till her sheet was tied in a knot, she dreamed she was packing for a long journey and couldn't find anything she wanted.

She woke early and padded into the kitchen. It wasn't too late. She could ride down to the barn before anyone else was awake and tell Billy it was all off. But what would she tell Mom?

She poured herself a glass of orange juice and looked out the kitchen window. It was going to be a scorcher of a day. Six hours till noon. She went and washed her hair and stood under the shower until Jim hammered at the door.

The morning dragged on, slower than any morning she could remember, but at last the clock in the hall struck noon. Mom was running the vacuum cleaner over Jim's floor, Dad and Jim were out and Grandpa was watching a game show, so only Susan saw the bus hurtle along the road at the end of the property. Only she saw a small figure suddenly appear under the arch of the main gate and plod slowly up the trail.

Here goes! She took a deep breath, went out onto the porch and waved. The small figure waved back. She went inside again and yelled over the roar of the vacuum, "Mom, he's here."

"Goodness. Here, put this thing away." Mom whipped off her apron and patted her hair smooth. "Do I look all right?"

"It's only cousin Bobbie, not the President, Mom." Susan bundled the vacuum away in the closet and followed her mother out onto the porch in time to hear her say, "So you're Bobbie Stevens. My, how you've grown! I believe you do take after your mother. Welcome to our home, Bobbie."

CHAPTER FIVE

This has definitely been the longest day in my life, thought Susan, as she flopped into bed with a groan that night. Various moments flashed back in their full horror. Lunch hadn't been too bad, with only Mom and Grandpa there, and she had been able to divert most of Mom's questions. Then she had whisked Billy out of the house and down to the barn, away from Mom. "We're just going to look at the old carousel."

Mom had laughed. "Zeke's Folly? Just don't let Irving Welty catch you playing in the barn, that's all." And Susan had spent the rest of the afternoon trying to drum into "Bobbie's" head that he'd better get used to drinking milk, since Mom was set on it for growing kids; and that it wasn't okay to spit on the floor either.

But they had to get back for dinner, with Dad and Jim as well as Mom and Grandpa, all focusing on the newcomer, like he was a long lost relative—which of course they believe he is, Susan thought. First off he'd started sniffing, and when she'd seen his hand go up to his nose she'd kicked him under the table. He'd caught on all right, and blown his nose lavishly on Mom's embroidered dinner napkin.

Mom's face! Susan almost giggled at the memory, though it had been really awful at the time. Mom had handled it pretty well, considering. She'd handed Bobbie a tissue and put the napkin to soak in cold water. "I hope you're not getting a cold" was all she'd said. Boy, if I'd ever pulled a trick like that, Susan thought, Mom would have *killed* me.

Then the questioning had started again.

"How are Alicia and Melissa? Big girls, I expect."

He'd nodded, his mouth full of lasagna.

"I suppose Alicia's in school."

Susan had mouthed "yes" at him, and he'd obediently replied "Yes, ma'am." So far so good, she thought, breathing a sigh of relief.

"And what grade are you in?"

"School? I done with all that stuff."

They'd all stared and Susan had tried to fill the gap with chatter. "What a kidder you are, Bobbie! Mom, he just means he's finished for *vacation*. Who wants to talk about *school* in the holidays?"

Then Jim got into the act. "D'you remember playing checkers with me when you were about six? How's your game now?"

"Checkers? Wha—? I guess I ain't played since. I c'n play gin rummy though. Johannes taught me."

"How nice," Mom had said feebly. "Who's Johannes, dear?"

"The old guy I. . .an old guy I know."

"You can give me a game, young fella," Grandpa had put in then and whisked Billy away right after dessert. Susan had wanted to hang around to keep an eye on things, but she was stuck with drying the dishes, sneaking over to the door between plates to listen to what was going on in the living room.

"Goodness, you're a slowpoke tonight." Mom rinsed the sink and dried her hands. "While you're finishing up I'm going to unpack Bobbie's things and make sure he's got everything he needs. One small bag for a month's visit? I just can't think what got into Marian sending him off like that."

"I can unpack for him. You needn't bo—" But Mom was gone, and Susan finished the dishes, hoping Mom wouldn't recognize the old suitcase or Jim's discarded tee-shirts.

She got into the living room just as Mom appeared. "Did your mother leave a phone number where she could be reached, Bobbie?"

"Phone? No, Ma'am."

"Oh, dear. How inconvenient. I would like to have called—just to say you'd arrived safely, of course," she added.

Now, lying in bed, Susan could hear her mother talking to Dad in the bedroom next to hers. "It's all so odd, Tom."

"What way?" Dad sounded sleepy.

"Every way, for land's sake! A phone call out of the blue. Pushing him on a bus without even talking to me; just leaving that odd message with Susan. So *abrupt*. It's just not like Marian. And you should see what she packed for him. A few shabby old clothes thrown in a case. Winter pajamas. Not even a spare pair of runners. And no brush and comb."

Darn, thought Susan. I thought I'd remembered everything.

Through the wall she heard Dad laugh. "You're

making a storm out of a breeze, Veronica. Maybe the young fella did his own packing."

"Well, maybe. But even so. Tom, you must have noticed. His manners are so. . .so *rough*."

"You mean using his napkin for a handkerchief. You should have seen your face!"

"Not only that. Everything about him. Not at all what you'd expect. I'm sure he wasn't like that last time we visited. And his father's a *dentist*. In New Hampshire. I'd never for a moment let Susan or Jim get away with it. It's all very well for you to laugh, Tom Patterson, but I just *know* something's wrong. You should be more concerned. After all, Marian's *your* sister."

Susan sat up in bed and strained her ears. Had Mom guessed? Could she have?

"Maybe she and David are having problems. Maybe they've sent Bobbie to us and left the girls with *his* relatives so they can work things out."

"Maybe there's nothing wrong at all and they just want a holiday together."

"Dumping the boy on a bus and sending him half across the country? He's only ten, Tom."

"Quit fussing, Veronica, and come to bed."

There was silence next door. Maybe Dad had been able to stop Mom from worrying, but Susan certainly couldn't. She lay awake biting her nails, which was a habit she'd gotten right out of when she was seven. Suppose Jim was grilling Billy right now? How'd he make out without her giving him signals when to say "yes" or "no"?

Billy lay stiff as a board between the clean smooth sheets. Thoughts raced around inside his head and his heart pounded like he was running from the cops again. He relived the ride, the carousel spinning faster and faster, so he could feel the wind of it lifting his hair. The heart-stopping moment of flying through the air. Then waking up to the alien smell of hay and barn dust. An empty land with a sky so wide there was nowhere to hide under it.

Nineteen ninety-three. Was it possible? Had he really travelled into the future? He recalled the small silver shape tearing across the sky. The monster aluminum-sided automobile that had thundered by as he waited in the ditch by the entrance to the farm. The "bus", Susan had called it. It had whipped the hair up on his head like the carousel ride, and left behind it a cloud of road dust clear back to the horizon.

The house didn't look like any house he'd ever seen. Not the rooming house where he'd lived with Dad, nor Mrs. Weingarten's crowded rooms. Certainly not the cosy frowziness of the old man's shack. This place had shiny white boxes everywhere, one you could cook on without putting in wood or coal, one as cold as an icebox, though there wasn't a block of ice in it. In the cellar was another box that washed clothes. How could a white cube wash clothes? And there was that other thing they called teevee. People talking and moving about, like they were right there inside the box behind the curved glass front. But how *could* they be?

Billy's stomach was full, almost uncomfortably so. He'd got clean clothes and his skin didn't itch. That shower was another amazing thing, the way the water came down, finer than rain and warm, and then ran away under the floor. He turned on his side, the rustle of sheets incredibly loud, and heard an echoing rustle from the bed across the room.

"You okay, Bobbie?" Jim whispered.

He lay rigid again, eyes tight shut, trying to make his breathing sound like he was asleep. There'd been too many questions already, and this Jim guy had looked at him kind of shifty a few times, like he suspected there was something wrong.

Wrong? Everything was wrong! He could see in his mind, close enough to reach out and touch, the tousled hair and beard of Johannes, his face blotchy red. He could hear his rough breathing, the catch in it when the pain caught him. Johannes needs me, he thought, panic clutching at his throat like a stone that hurt when he tried to swallow. He could *die* without me there to look after him. And who's to take the tickets and run the carousel when he's sick? Who's to get his special medicine from old Mrs. Weingarten? He remembered, then, how he'd actually thought of taking the old man's money and running off. He squirmed under the covers.

The window curtain blew and an unfamiliar breeze, warm but unfriendly, smelling of nothing but cleanness, wafted into the room. In his memory was the familiar frowsty smell in the little hut, a comfortable mixture of sweat, coal oil, old fried bacon and beans. He longed for the familiar scratchiness of the blanket in which he slept, smelling of himself, warm, friendly. The stone in his throat seemed to swell and swell until it filled his whole throat and suddenly exploded into a sob. He screwed up his eyes tight and bit on the edge of the sheet.

"We're going down to the barn again," Susan said first thing in the morning, hoping to forestall any plans Mom might be hatching.

"Oh, I thought we'd visit—"

"Mom, please."

"Why do you want to go down there? You're only asking for trouble. That piece of land belongs to Irving Welty, as you well know."

"But the carousel's ours. And we want to clean the carousel animals."

"Why now? You've never been interested before. And I'm not sure it's a healthy way to spend the summer, cooped up in a stuffy barn."

"Bobbie's interested. And there's plenty of ventilation with the door open. Don't *fuss,* Mom. Come on, Bobbie, let's brush our teeth and get going."

"But I brushed them yester—"

"What a kidder you are. C'mon." She dragged him out of the room.

They were busy inspecting the boiler with a flashlight when a shadow blocked the light from the door.

"Who's that? Oh, it's only you, Jim. Gee, you scared me. I thought for sure it was Mr. Welty after our hides. Or that creep George. What d'you want anyway?"

"A private talk. Away from Mom and Dad."

"Can't it wait? We're kind of busy."

"Oh, sure. It *could* wait till dinner. I could ask you a whole bunch of embarrassing questions in front of the grown-ups."

"Okay, okay. I guess you'd better come in."

"What are you two doing here anyway? I thought you were going to clean the animals." Jim crossed the platform and dropped down into the centre where the drive mechanism stood.

"Just playing around."

"With kerosene. And oily rags. D'you want to burn the barn down?"

"Course not. I know exactly what I'm doing, Jim Patterson. We've been cleaning up the engine a bit, that's all. I'll take out the kerosene and the rags when we leave."

"Haven't looked at this old thing in years." Jim put his hand on the boiler. "Wonder if you could still get up a head of steam on it. Could be fun to try some day."

"That's what we're aiming to do."

"You two? Uh-huh. Either it'll leak like a sieve and get you nowhere, or it'll hold pressure and you'll blow yourselves up. You can't mess around with steam."

"I suppose *you* could do it right, smartie?"

"Maybe I could." He looked at them. "Maybe I *will*. If you'll tell me who this kid is. 'Cause he sure isn't Bobbie Stevens." He pulled a crumpled piece of paper from his pocket.

"What are you talking about?" She snatched the paper. "Where d'you get this?"

"Outta your wastebasket. You're smart, little sister, but not smart enough. You should have destroyed the evidence."

"Don't you call me little sister. Poking around in my room. Honestly! Anyway, this isn't anything important. It. . .it's only the original of Aunt Marian's phone message. I copied it out again so Mom could read my writing."

"Nice try! Three copies? Different wording each time too. As for you, young man." Jim caught Billy by the shoulders and turned him around to face him. "How come you got off the bus when it never even slowed down?"

"How d'you know it didn't?" Susan snapped, before Billy could speak. "You couldn't possibly have seen it from where you and Dad were working yesterday."

"I could sure hear it. Yesterday was real quiet, not a

breath of wind, remember? The bus went right on by.
So who are you, young fella?"

"Billy," he muttered.

"Billy who?"

"Just Billy."

"Leave him alone, Jim. He's a friend of mine, okay?
He's got no family. Nowhere to stay. I found him in the
barn. He'd banged his head. He couldn't stay down
here, so I sort of pretended he was Bobbie Stevens."

"You sort of. . .? Brilliant! Susan, where's your
brain? He arrives out of nowhere. You don't know
who he really is. Could be a runaway from juvenile
detention or something like that. I bet you don't even
know where he's come from. . ."

"I do too."

"Okay, where?"

"Not telling."

"Then I'm going to tell Mom that he's not Bobbie
Stevens, and *you* can explain why you lied to her."

"You can't. Please, Jim. I'll do anything. Only don't tell."

"Who is he, then? Honestly?"

"I come on the carousel," Billy said abruptly.

Jim stared from one to the other. "*Two* kids with a
twisted sense of humour. All I need."

"I *did*. Johannes said 'go too fast and it'll spin you
off into tomorrow.' And it *did*. Now it's all broke and I
can't get back."

"Hey, look, don't cry. You're not kidding? You really
mean it, don't you? You got here on the carousel?
This carousel."

"Didn't look like this then. All new and shiny, it
was. And not in a dirty old barn neither. In the gardens." Billy sniffed and wiped his nose on his arm.
"With Johannes."

"The old man who taught you gin rummy?"

"Yeah. And he's real sick. I didn't ought to have left him like I did. I thought I'd be gone no time at all. Mister, I *gotta* get back."

"Back where?"

"Like I said, the city."

Jim stared at him and licked his lips, as if his mouth was suddenly dry. "What did you mean: 'the carousel'd spin you off into *tomorrow*'? When were you in the city?"

" 'Twere summer, like now. And the moon was full too. But it were nineteen hundred oh-eight."

"Right!"

"Jim, it's true. He was born just after the Klondike gold rush and he's never seen a zipper or a shower or anything."

"Wow!" Jim sat down on the edge of the platform. He looked at Billy, reached out and touched him. "Wow!" he said again.

"You mean you believe us, Jim?"

"I guess so. I don't think even you could have made up anything so outrageous. In a way it kinda makes sense. I've heard of people falling back into the past. There were two old ladies visiting France who found themselves at Versailles at the end of the eighteenth century, everyone in costume with wigs and things. That's a true story, not science fiction. So maybe one can fall into the future."

"The future?" Susan stared out the barn door. "I was thinking about Billy living in the *past*, not us living in the future. That's really spooky."

"Not really. If you think about it, our present will be someone else's past. Come to that, when we're old and grey, that's what today'll be. Our past."

"You're talking and talking, but aren't you never going to help me get *back*?"

"Okay, Billy. Don't get steamed up. What you're saying happened is, the carousel went too fast and spun you off here, into your future. Is that right?"

"Yessir."

"How come no one else came too—all the people riding the other animals? Why only you?"

"Huh? Oh, I was on me own. It were the middle of the night. Johannes was sleeping when I snuck out. He used to ride it, see. It was his secret. But I found out how it worked and I had to try. Just the once. To see what he saw. But it ain't the same. And he got back safe right away." He sniffed again.

"So how did it work?"

"There's a governor, here, you see. Push it aside and she goes faster and faster."

Jim shook his head. "That doesn't make sense. It should have blown apart. There must be more to it than that. Some kind of magic. That must have been the old man's secret. The magic."

"He didn't say nothing about magic. When I spied him, first time I got to the gardens, I told him what I seen and he said I'd been dreaming. But I weren't. 'Cause I saw him ride another night, when he thought I were asleep. But the moonlight woke me up. It were full moon or pretty near."

"Maybe that's got something to do with it. The full moon. Like tides. If that's true, we'll have to get this thing moving before the next full moon. Four weeks. It isn't long."

"Jim, you don't really believe that magic and the full moon and stuff like that made the carousel into a time machine? It's not scientific."

"Magic's just a word for what scientists don't understand yet. Anyway, the plain fact is Billy's here instead of in nineteen hundred and eight, and there's got to be some explanation for that. Maybe it's got something to do with magnetic fields," he added vaguely.

"You're talking and talking, all them jaw-breaking words. But what's it mean? How'm I going to get home?" Billy wailed.

"Take it easy, fella. We'll make a plan. First off, we've got to start by cleaning out all the pipes, make sure they're not blocked. And see that the boiler's sound, with no leaks. Then we'll have to oil the bearings and gears and make sure the platform's sitting true." Jim ran his hand through his hair. "Some job. All in a month!"

"You mean you're going to help us, Jim? And you won't tell Mom and Dad?"

"If I don't help you'll probably blow yourselves up. But it's going to take all our cunning to do this without the parents interfering. And they'd *never* believe Billy's story."

"You're going to fix it so I can go home, mister?"

"Only if you call me Jim. And remember to use a tissue to blow your nose. I can't believe I'm saying this—I sound like Mom! The toughest part for me is how to get out of fence fixing. Dad's bound and determined this is the summer I'm going to learn to love farming. And harvest time's close."

"Tell him we're going to restore the carousel as a summer project. Maybe he'll go for it."

It worked, sort of. Except for worrying about Irving Welty.

"It's *our* carousel. Great-grandpa bought it years and years ago."

"But the barn's on Mr. Welty's land. There's no getting away from that. And you know what a curmudgeon *he* is," Jim reminded Susan. "Why, he hasn't even passed the time of day with Grandpa in years, has he, Gramps?"

Susan stared accusingly at her grandfather. "So what's wrong with you two, anyway?"

He chuckled. "You may well ask! It began back in twenty-eight, when my dad got wind of the city fathers selling their carousel and buying one of those newfangled ones that go up and down as well as round and round. He thought what a great thing it'd be for the county if we had our very own carousel. He was always an independent son of a gun, so, when it came up for auction he put in a bid for it, without telling anyone else, and he found he'd bought himself a genuine carousel. But he hadn't reckoned on the shipping costs or needing somewhere to store it once he'd got it here, and folks in town wanted no part of it."

"Is that where Irving Welty came in?"

"No, Susan, not Irving. His daddy, Charlie Welty. My dad, that's Zeke Patterson, persuaded Charlie to pay the shipping charges, and between them they built the big round barn to house it, on that piece of Welty land right down by the road. Well, they got it all put together and running fine, and they planned a grand opening for July the Fourth, 1928. Just about everyone in the county and beyond came to see. And the town band and all."

"You too, Grandpa?"

"Of course. I was about eight years old then. Never forget that day. No sir! My dad put me up on the lead horse, handsome big charger it was, with armour on its head and—"

"Chain mail down its neck and all around," Billy put in eagerly.

"How in the world'd you know about that, young Bobbie?"

"Why, I. . ."

"We already started cleaning up the animals, Grandpa, like we told you," Susan interrupted hastily.

"So you did. Anyway, my dad put me up on the lead horse, and everyone climbed on the other animals. The band played a big fanfare and we were all set to go when the trouble started. Charlie, who was seeing to the drive mechanism, looked through the panels and saw me on that horse. 'Now just a darn minute,' he yelled, or words to that effect, and he tromped across the platform and whisked me off that horse faster than you could spit. Then he pops Irving on it. Irving was about the same age I was. Then he goes back to start the carousel up. But meantime, my dad's picked Irving off and put me up again on the lead horse. So Charlie comes busting back and—to cut a long story short, there were the two of them, trying to outface each other, madder'n hornets on a hot day, and there's Irving and me getting bounced on and off that horse till we were sore."

"So what happened in the end?"

"Neither of them would start the carousel with the other kid on the lead horse, and in the end everyone went home mad at the Weltys *and* the Pattersons, and we haven't had much to do with each other since that July the Fourth."

"Grandpa, that's the most ridiculous story I *ever* heard. I can't believe you'd be enemies over a little thing like that!"

"Well now, Susan, you just hold on a minute. It wasn't only the carousel. It was like. . .like a creek getting blocked up and flooding. It doesn't happen all at once. A bit of this and a bit of that. I guess it really began before I was born, when my ma and pa came out homesteading to Colorado, and the Weltys were running cattle over the range. That made for hard feelings at the time, but they got patched up, and the Weltys settled down next to us. But I guess just about every grudge of the previous eighteen years got aired that day they started up the carousel."

"They did run it, didn't they? People came from all over?"

Grandpa shook his head. "Wasn't too long after that the banks collapsed and the depression started. Nobody'd got the time or money for carousels. But the real problem was my pa wouldn't let Charlie lay a hand on the carousel he'd paid for, and Charlie wouldn't let my pa set foot on his land. It was a stand-off."

"I still think it's the silliest story I've ever heard," Susan said crossly. "It's about time we buried the hatchet and got the carousel going again."

"I wouldn't say no to that," Grandpa admitted.

"But go easy, kids," Dad advised. "Old Irving Welty's a bit of a curmudgeon. His arthritis doesn't help. And if you trespass on his land you're in the wrong."

"But you get on okay with Sam Welty, don't you, Dad? And it's him that runs their place, not his pa."

"What about young George?" Jim said later to Susan. "He's an okay kid."

"Jim, he's a creep!"

"Honestly, Susan!"

"Well, he is. He's a pain! He's. . .Anyway, I'd just like to see the Weltys stop us!"

"Okay, but we'd better just be careful, that's all. And the first thing we'd better do is check out that boiler. Because if it leaks, forget it. No use wasting time on anything else." Jim spoke briskly, taking charge as usual.

Susan bit her lip. It'd been fun having Billy as her very own secret. But, to be fair, she'd probably not get anywhere without Jim's help. And it wasn't a *game*, though it was an adventure. Billy had to get home. "Okay," she said at last. "It's going to take a lot of water. How'll we manage it?"

"Fill some old oil drums, I guess. And haul them down to the road in the truck."

It hadn't sounded too tough, but they found that the drums weighed a ton, even when they were only half full, and getting them up the ramp onto the back of the truck was no joke. But it was done at last, and Jim drove down the track from the house to the highway and north to the barn.

"We sure are conspicuous," Susan remarked as they jolted along.

"We won't need the truck after today, and Irving Welty's not going to come riding down to the bottom of his property, not with his arthritis. Here we are."

Unloading the full drums wasn't as bad as loading them up had been, but once they were all safely inside the barn there was another hurdle. "There's no way we can haul them up on the platform and across to the boiler. The animals are too close together. We could knock off a leg or do some other damage."

"Those animals are pretty well shot anyway." Jim wiped the sweat off his forehead with his sleeve. "What do you suggest, Susan?"

"You're not giving up again, are you?" Billy asked anxiously.

"Course not. I guess we'll just have to have a bucket brigade, that's all. Feed buckets'll do. I'll go up to the stable and get some. You two can start checking pipes and joints and stuff like that," Susan added vaguely.

She tied her hat under her chin and set off along

the path between their land and the Weltys'. The sun blazed down out of a sky so bright she had to squint her eyes as she walked. It had taken them far longer than she'd thought to fill and haul the water drums. "I'll ride Judy back," she said aloud, and the grasshoppers whirred and clicked and threw themselves against her legs in reply.

Almost noon, she thought, and detoured to the house to make lunch for the three of them. Mom bustled in, her head tied up in a scarf. "How hot you look. Wouldn't you rather stay home? You can help me turn out the cellar. It's lovely and cool down there."

"It's a great offer, but no thanks, Mom." She stuffed beef and tomato sandwiches, pickles, pop and apples into a backpack. "I'm off. Don't wear yourself out."

"Nor you either, in that heat!"

She slung three feed pails from Judy's saddle and walked the mare down to the barn. It was cooler sitting up high on her back, with a bit of a breeze to fan the sweat off her face and neck. She brought Judy right into the barn, out of the sun, and hitched her near the door. Then they began the bucket line, Susan filling each pail, passing it on to Billy, who scurried across the platform to give it to Jim and pick up the empty one and bring it back to her.

"That's enough, I think," Jim said after a while.

"Just as well. That's the bottom of the last barrel." Susan straightened up and groaned. "How's it holding?"

"Seems okay."

"Course it is." Billy put in. "I coulda told you that."

"It's been sitting here unused for sixty-five *years*, Billy."

He shivered, in spite of the heat, and his small face

looked paler than ever. "Can't seem to take it in. Not really. And the poor animals." He ran a hand down the neck of the Indian pony. "Look at these reins. All rotted, they are."

"It'll be okay, Billy. We'll get you back to where the carousel's all new and shiny. Let's relax and eat lunch, and figure out what to do next."

They sat on the edge of the platform, eating their lunch.

"You going to start her up now, Jim?"

"Hold on, Billy. We've got a long way to go before that."

"I gotta get back." Billy sprayed crumbs as he protested. "It's been two nights and a day'n a half I been gone. Johannes is gonna think I run off."

"I've been thinking about that." Jim took a long drink of pop. "Did your friend ever tell you how long he was away when *he* rode the carousel?"

"It wasn't no time at all. Like I told you afore, the carousel went all misty, and then it come back, with the old man still astride the leader here."

"I know that's what *you* saw, Billy. What I want to know is what Johannes was experiencing in those few seconds."

Billy looked blank.

"I get it," Susan interrupted. "Look, Billy, maybe it seemed to Johannes that he'd been away for ages, even though it was really only a few seconds. Did he tell you about what he saw or did?"

Billy shook his head. "It were a secret. But he was rambling, the other night—I mean, before I come here—about what he'd seen. That's funny. He were talking like he'd been a while looking, but it were just a blink of an eye. But what's the time got to do with me getting back?"

"Time's relative. How fast or slow it goes depends on where you're standing."

"Huh?"

"Imagine Johannes was watching while you rode the carousel the night before last. . ."

"But he *weren't*. I *told* you, he was sick abed."

"We know that, Billy," Susan said impatiently. "Just pretend, okay? Go on, Jim."

"Yeah, pretend he's watching you. What'll he see?"

"You mean like *I* saw? The carousel going fast and faster. Then misty, like it weren't there any more. Gone. Then misty again and slowing down. . ."

"With you on the pony's back!" Jim finished triumphantly.

"But. . ." Billy stopped and scratched his head. "You mean, it don't matter how long I stay here? Back *home* it'll still be the night afore last until I get back."

"Attaboy! You've got it." Jim got up and gave his apple core to Judy. "Time we got on to the next stage, to check all the pipes and fittings." He crossed the platform and dropped down into the centre.

"C'n I give my apple core to the horse too?"

"Sure. Just hold it out on the flat of your hand. She won't bite."

"Tickles." Billy chuckled as Judy's soft lips mouthed the core. "I'd like to look after real horses some day. Maybe drive a dray. It's a good living doing that, I've heard, though Johannes says them automobiles are going to take over."

"He's right. Even on farms we only—Jim, what's the matter?"

He stood above them on the platform, his right hand outstretched. It gleamed wet in the light from the open door.

"Oh, Jim!" Susan scrambled over to the boiler. "But it looks fine."

"The bottom seam."

"It's not *really* leaking. Just sweating a bit."

Jim shook his head. "The water's not just going to be sitting there. It'll be under pressure—a whole lot of pressure if we're to get this thing going fast. It'd blow apart long before we got there."

Susan slumped down onto the platform. "Whatever are we going to do now?"

Billy looked from brother to sister. Strangers really, these two from so far into the future they weren't even going to get *born* for seventy years. He couldn't make sense of what Jim said, but the expressions on their faces told him the truth.

"It ain't going to work, that's it?"

"Not with this boiler. I'm sorry, Billy."

"What'm I going to do. I gotta get back. I can't stop *here*."

When Susan took his hand she felt warm and kind of comforting. He'd got the shivers, like when he had to sleep out in the winter.

"Maybe you should stay here, Billy," she said. "It's a better world than yours. There's more to eat. And a warm bed. If you get sick there's antibiotics to make you better fast. If Johannes were here the doctors'd make him better in no time at all. And you could go to school, maybe on to college. Better than just looking after horses."

He pulled his hand away. "You don't understand. The grub's good, yeah. And these clothes. Though I don't go for all this washing and toothbrushing. Wears out your skin. But that ain't what's important. I don't belong here. Never will."

"Don't you think you'd get used to it? It'd be like

emigrating from another country. You're emigrating from another time, that's all."

Despair flooded Billy's heart. If they started trying to persuade him to *stay*, then they wouldn't even *try* to get the carousel working again. They didn't know what it felt like to be trapped, and he didn't have the words to tell them.

"I can't leave Johannes."

"He's not family, is he? Just a friend."

Just a friend. With a flush of guilt Billy remembered how he'd thought of taking Johannes's savings cache and heading off on his own. Even as he'd gone for the "medicine" he'd thought that. His treachery burned into him like a hot coal. "That's it, ain't it?" he burst out. "He's a *friend*. He's the only one ever looked out for me after me dad went off. How can I go off and leave him when he's sick and old? And all your jaw-breaking words about time being relative and all that and Johannes seeing me come back the night afore last, that don't mean nothing, 'cause if I can't get back he ain't never going to see me."

Jim jumped from the platform and wiped his wet hand on his jeans. "That's an interesting point. What do you think, Susan? What would Billy see when the carousel slowed down? Come to that, what's going to make the carousel slow down ever, if Billy here isn't aboard?"

"Darn it, Jim, why do you have to be so *intellectual*? Can't you see what Billy's going through?"

"I'm not just being theoretical. I'm getting somewhere. Listen, you two. We know the carousel must have slowed down and stopped again the night before last back in nineteen hundred and eight—"

"How do we know that?" Susan interrupted.

"Because it had to have been there next morning

and all the other mornings, because we know the carousel went on existing right through to nineteen twenty-eight when Great-grandpa Zeke Patterson bought it and brought it here."

"You mean, if it never returned to nineteen oh-eight it couldn't be here now? I get it."

"I don't. It's just words. Why don't you do something? Help me get back."

"It's not just words, Bobbie. I'm proving that the carousel *does* go back to being its normal self in nineteen hundred and eight. Therefore we are going to be able to make it happen."

"Even if the boiler don't work?"

"Even then."

"That's all very fine and philosophical, Jim Patterson, but how on earth are we going to do it?"

"I don't know yet, but I'll think of something."

"We'd better hurry up. We've got to get it running by the next full moon."

Jim whistled between his teeth. "Two deadlines then."

"What's the other?"

"Bobbie Stevens is going to have to return to his loving family back east, before someone catches us out. Which'll be a whole lot sooner than the next full moon if we keep calling him Billy."

"But that's me name."

"Not here it isn't. You're Bobbie Stevens and don't you forget it. You, too, Susan."

"Okay, Jim boss. So what are we going to do now?"

"One thing we've got to do is clean up under the platform—make sure there's nothing to get in the way of its movement, like rats' nests."

"Ugh." Susan shuddered. "How'll we do that?"

"You need a long bit of wood that pokes right through," Billy put in. "Clean it out that way."

They both stared. "Of course. You looked after this carousel, didn't you?"

"Not *this*'n. Mine's a beauty. All shiny paint and bright eyes. And the reins and stirrup straps lovely soft leather. I cleaned them up every day. This un's horrible."

Susan rubbed her arms as if she were suddenly goose-pimply. "It's like family photographs, isn't it? I mean looking at Grandpa when he was a cute little baby. Then in uniform after Pearl Harbor. And now he's an old man with a crippled hip and arm. But if you think about it, all the Luke Pattersons exist together: the baby, the soldier, the old man. But in different times."

"I see what you mean, Susan. The carousel's like that. The carousel Bobbie remembers is like Grandpa as a baby. And the one Great-grandpa Zeke bought is the soldier. And this. . ."

As they looked silently at the broken-down carousel, the horses and menagerie animals worn and broken, the leathers rotted, their heads bowed as if they were ashamed of their condition, Judy suddenly stamped her foot and nickered. They all turned. A shadow crossed the band of light on the barn floor.

"Who's that in there?"

"Jim Patterson. What's it to you?"

"You're on my land, young man, that's what it is to me. Now clear off, all of you."

"Mr. Welty!" Susan cried out in dismay. "We're not doing any harm. And it *is* our carousel."

Sam Welty was a big man, much bulkier than Dad. Right now he seemed to swell up even bigger. "On *our* land," was all he said and went on standing there, legs apart, hands on hips.

"Come on, Sue," Jim muttered. "Don't make an issue of it. Let's go."

They hauled the empty drums and pails out of the barn and loaded them on the truck. Susan took Judy's bridle and led her out of the barn. Sam Welty shut the door behind them. "Reckon I'd better put a padlock on this."

Susan opened her mouth, swallowed, and shut it again. She slung the backpack across her shoulders and mounted Judy. "See you up at the house, boys." She walked Judy along the fence line that separated the Patterson and Welty properties, longing to gallop her, get rid of her anger; but it wouldn't be fair to Judy. Not in this heat.

Now what were they going to do? It was all very well for Jim to talk about how the carousel being here proved that it did go back to Billy's time, but that was all words, wasn't it? When you got down to *facts*, they were these: The drive mechanism wouldn't work without steam, and they weren't going to get any steam because the boiler leaked. And Sam Welty wouldn't let them near the carousel again anyway. Billy was trapped.

CHAPTER SIX

"You're back early. Too hot for you down in that old barn, I bet. There's lemonade in the fridge."

Susan got out the pitcher and poured for them all. Mom had put mint leaves in the lemonade, which tasted tangy fresh. The ice cubes nudged against her lips. Some of her hot anger cooled. "Sam Welty came down and threw us out, Mom. It's not fair. He's no right."

Grandpa was sitting at the kitchen table snapping beans for dinner. He chuckled. "Warned you, didn't I?"

Susan felt herself getting mad again. "What right has he got to interfere? We weren't doing anything wrong. And it *is* our carousel."

"Cool it, Sue," Jim muttered. "We'll work out something."

"Bobbie, how pale you are!" Mom interrupted

before she could explode. "I do hope you're not sickening for something." She put a hand to his head. "Why don't you go lie down before supper? Too much heat, and you're not accustomed, being an easterner."

He bolted from the room and Susan heard him sniffing as he ran down the passage. She bit her lip. It was all very well for Jim to be philosophical, but something drastic was going to have to be done.

She sat silent right through dinner, wondering what she could do. She didn't notice that Jim and Billy were equally silent until Grandpa suddenly exploded. "Tarnation, it's like a morgue in here! What's got into you kids?"

"Nothing, Grandpa."

"Don't give me 'nothing'. I suppose you're sulking over the Weltys. Well, I did warn you."

"We're not *sulking*. It's just. . ." Susan swallowed. How could she possibly explain? They'd never believe the truth of Billy being trapped in the wrong time.

Mom got up to clear the plates. "Bobbie, you've hardly touched your food! Do you feel ill?"

"Just not hungry, ma'am."

"Me neither." Susan pushed back her chair. "Please may I be excused? I'd like to exercise Judy now it's a bit cooler."

"But there's lemon meringue pie for dessert," Mom exclaimed.

"Maybe later, okay?"

"Well, I'll have a slice of pie, thank you, Veronica. And I bet Dad will. You kids must be nuts," their father said.

Susan pulled on her boots and slid out of the house.

"Where do you think you're heading off to? Wait for Bobbie and me. We've got to make a plan."

"It's all just words with you. What we need's a bit of action." She stalked into the stable and began to saddle up Judy.

Jim followed her, with Billy coming slowly behind. "Bobbie's really upset," he said quietly. "He was howling his eyes out before supper. Like a little kid."

"He's got something to cry about, hasn't he? How'd you feel if you were stuck in someone else's time?" Susan swung herself up into the saddle.

"Well, why don't you stick around and help cheer him up?"

"You can do that, Jim Patterson. I've got more important things in mind." She turned Judy towards the track that led to the northern fence.

"You're not going back to the barn, are you? That's dumb. You'll just get in trouble and what's the use anyway. *Sue!*"

She walked Judy along the track, ignoring Jim's voice behind her. Would Sam Welty really do as he'd threatened and put a padlock on the barn door? But whether he planned to or not, something had to be done.

Once she reached the highway she turned north and trotted Judy along the grassy shoulder towards the entrance to the Welty place. Her heart thumped in rhythm to the mare's gait and she felt out of breath and—yes, she had to admit it—scared. Was Irving Welty really the ogre he'd been made out to be?

Maybe it won't be too bad, she told herself firmly, as she turned under the wooden archway with the Welty brand on it. After all, they can't eat me, can they? She slowed Judy to a walk, trying to order in her mind what it was she wanted to say. Her heart thumped and she licked her dry lips.

Now the house was in sight, a low sprawling house

not much different from theirs. How weird that she'd never been here before, never been on Welty property—except for the barn, of course—even though they'd been neighbours since before she was born, and she'd ridden the same school bus with George Welty every year.

He'll be there, she suddenly realised, and she almost turned back. Suppose she made a total idiot of herself in front of George? He'd tell the other guys in their grade. They'd all laugh at her.

Just then someone came out onto the porch, someone in the same kind of housedress Mom wore, and it was too late to turn back. She had to walk Judy up to the porch, dismount and hitch her to the porch rail with the enemy's eyes on her.

Mrs. Sam Welty said in a very ordinary voice—not as if she were repelling an invader—"Why, it's Susan Patterson, isn't it? Did you want to see George? He's right inside."

Susan swallowed and wiped her sweaty hands against her jeans. "No, ma'am. It's Mr. Irving Welty I've come to see. If it's convenient, that is?"

Mrs. Welty stared at her. *No wonder*, thought Susan miserably. *It's like Daniel inviting himself into the lion's den.* "I suppose so," she said slowly. "He doesn't get many visitors. His arthritis bothers him a lot these days. Why don't you just wait on the porch and I'll go and see if he's up to company."

"Thank you, ma'am." Susan stood on the wide porch and stared at the patchwork cushions on the glider. They were the same log-cabin pattern that was on the quilt on Grandpa's bed.

The screen door squeaked and banged and she looked up. But it was George, lounging against the door frame, staring at her.

"Hi. So what are you doing here?"

"Hi. Waiting to talk to your grandfather." She felt her cheeks grow hot.

"Why in the world'd you want to do that? His temper's worse than usual, I warn you."

"I. . .I've got a message."

"Mr. Bell invented the telephone a while back. Real good for messages."

"This is. . .this is personal." *Darn it*, she thought. *Why don't you go away and quit bugging me. I can't remember what I was going to say. I wish I hadn't come. I can't handle this.*

The screen squeaked again. "My father-in-law will see you now, Susan. Won't you come in?"

George was still blocking the doorway. She looked up at him and stuck out her chin. "Excuse *me*."

He moved to one side. "Good luck." He had a grin right across his freckled face. She brushed by without looking at him and followed Mrs. Welty into the lion's den.

Mr. Irving Welty and his son Sam were in the living room. Each was sitting on a recliner with his feet up, each with a can of beer in his hand. The television was blaring. "The Atlanta Braves at Cincinnati," Sam Welty said without taking his eyes off the screen. "So you've come to apologize, have you, young lady?"

Susan stared. "Apologize? What for?"

"For trespassing, of course."

As she stared, open mouthed, everything she wanted to say forgotten, she saw the eyes of the old man swivel towards her and then back to the screen. His hands were badly swollen and twisted with arthritis; she noticed that it took both hands to hold his beer can. He was hunched awkwardly in his recliner, and his long legs—he must once have been way taller than Grandpa—were thin as pea sticks.

"Well?"

"No, sir. I didn't come over to apologize. I figure we'd every right to be down there since it was *our* carousel. I came to say something to Mr. Irving Welty, please."

The pale blue eyes swivelled towards her again and then back to the green of the diamond. He didn't say a word. Susan swallowed. "Look, if you're busy, I'll come back another time."

"Suit yourself." Sam Welty watched the game.

Susan turned towards the door and then turned back again. *If I don't do it now*, she thought, *I'll never get up the nerve again.*

"Mr. Welty, you know my grandfather," she said firmly, standing close to the television, so that she could look Irving Welty in the eye, even if he wouldn't look at her. "He just told me the story about when you were little boys and your daddies quarrelled."

The corner of the old man's mouth twitched in a small humourless smile. "Never did see eye to eye, my dad and Zeke Patterson."

Encouraged by this small response, Susan plunged on. "It was the July Fourth in the year when the carousel was supposed to start. And my grandpa says you haven't spoken since. And. . .well. . .I came to say: isn't it kind of stupid and couldn't our families be friends again?"

The blue eyes were fastened on her now, and they weren't watery any longer. They were like icicles, piercing her through. She swallowed nervously. From the television beside her a man extolled the virtues of the brand of beer the Weltys were drinking. The ad promoted happy, family, party feelings, with everyone laughing together, like the beer was a magic potion. She wish it were. She wish it'd warm up these two.

Irving Welty put his beer can down beside him and used both hands to lever himself up in his chair. "You Pattersons are pretty glib talkers. Always were. Talked us out of our range land. Talked yourself into fencing the land with the best water in the county. Talked my pa out of good money to help buy that fool carousel. Talked him outta a piece of our land to put up the barn to house it. Now you're talking good neighbourliness? And I'm asking myself: why?"

"Because it's a shame not to be friends."

"Nothing to do with that blame carousel my son saw you playing with this very afternoon?"

"Well, yes, that's part of it," Susan stammered, her cheeks hot. "We thought it'd be a great scheme to restore it, get it running again."

"Why now? Why not any time in these last fifty years?"

"My grandpa said it was built in 1905—that'd make it ninety years old in two years. We thought it'd be a great idea to celebrate. . ." Susan's voice faded at the expression on Irving Welty's face.

"Poppycock!" the old man snapped. His body might be crippled up, but his voice was strong enough to drown out the commercials. "You Pattersons are up to something, that's what. Sneaking down to the barn all hours of the day and night. Testing that there boiler. You were planning to get her going on your own, weren't you? Grab all the glory for yourselves, like Zeke Patterson tried to do last time, only my daddy was a match for him."

"It's not like that, honest. It—"

"Then why didn't you come up here and talk to me nice before trespassing on our land?"

"I guess I didn't think it was. . .well. . .important."

The old man laughed. "Not important? Course it's important, or you wouldn't be up here now, trying to sweet-talk me into letting you back into the barn. Seems to me you Pattersons haven't changed all that much in three generations. Still sneaky. So you can go home and tell your daddy and Luke Patterson that there's no deal. That there carousel's on our land and if there's any more trouble, like you trespassing again, I'll get my son here and the boys to burn it down, and that'll be an end to it."

"You can't do that!" Susan clasped her hands together. "Not possibly."

"Why not? It's on my land. I can do what I want with it."

"But. . ." Susan stopped and bit her lip. *I can't tell him the carousel's a time machine. That Billy'll be trapped eighty-five years in his future.*

"Well? Persuade me."

"It's your land, Mr. Welty, but the carousel is *ours*."

The old man chuckled, a sound like dry branches rubbing together. "You play chess, miss?"

"Chess? No, sir."

"Have you heard of 'stalemate'? That's what we've got here. Stalemate. And I'm not surrendering. No, sirree. I'll play till you Pattersons turn blue. Now, I'll thank you to get off my property."

Susan bolted out of the door and through the kitchen, muttering "goodnight" to Mrs. Welty, who was putting away the dinner dishes. She pushed through the screen door and let it slam behind her. George followed her.

"Well, look at you. Red as a beet. I don't have to bet who won that argument."

"Your grandfather's so. . .so. . ." Susan spluttered.

"Go on."

"Oh, forget it, George Welty. You're all impossible." She unhitched Judy so roughly that the mare skittered back on her hooves and sidled nervously around.

"Want a hand mounting her?"

"Oh, hush up!" Susan managed to soothe Judy and finally cantered down the drive, thankful for the breeze that cooled her flaming cheeks. *What an idiot I made of myself in there*, she thought. *All for nothing. And I bet George Welty'll never forget it. He'll make my life at school even more miserable than before, the creep.*

She reached the road and slowed Judy to a walk. The barn came into sight. Her anger at the Weltys subsided. *What about Billy? What on earth am I going to tell him?*

"Well, we're just going to have to go ahead in spite of the Weltys," Jim said calmly, when Susan told him what she'd done. "We'll just have to be a whole lot more careful, that's all. We'll keep a lookout, so they don't sneak up and catch us working on the carousel. You sure had a nerve going over there."

"It was dumb," Susan said miserably. "I thought talking them into being friends again was such a great idea. But I've just made things worse, and now they suspect we're up to something."

"We've got it out in the open, that's all."

"But what are we going to tell Billy?"

"The truth, of course. He's a big boy."

"But. . ." Susan shivered. She was sitting up in bed, her arms linked around her knees, while Jim sprawled at the end of her bed. This late-night conference was the first chance they'd had to be alone.

"Look, Sue, the Weltys are the least of our worries. How to get the drive mechanism working is far more of a problem."

"And so little time. That is, if the full moon *is* important. We don't know that, of course."

"Full moon or not, Mom's going to expect 'Bobbie' to go back to New Hampshire in a month." Jim suddenly chuckled. "Of course, Aunt Marian could phone Mom any day and blow your story."

"Thanks a lot, Jim Patterson. Now I've got three things to worry about, as if one wasn't enough." Susan's voice rose.

There was a knock on the wall. "Stop chattering, you two. It's getting late."

"Don't worry," Jim whispered. "Remember the carousel *must* have got back to the amusement gardens in 1908 in order for Great-grandpa to have bought it in 1928." With that consoling thought he slipped out of the room.

Except it doesn't console me, Susan thought, as she pounded her pillow and tried to sleep. Jim's philosophy didn't really help with the immediate problem of dealing with the boiler *and* the Weltys. Her mother's words echoed through her head. *It's getting late.*

They sneaked down to the barn next morning, keeping low among the tall grass so no Weltys would see them. "Like spies or something," said Susan crossly. "Like we had no rights."

"I've been thinking," said Jim. "It doesn't really matter what kind of engine we use to get the carousel started. It doesn't have to be *steam*."

"But it was steam back in 1908."

"I know. But at this end of time, here in 1993, all we've really got to do is give the platform a big enough push to spin it back to Billy's time. And I think we could do that with an ordinary diesel motor."

"Could you link it up to the carousel drive?"

"I don't see why not. I bet I can work it out."

"*Okay!* What can Billy and I do to help?"

"You're good at drawing, Susan. Maybe you could sketch the drive mechanism, so I've got something to work on. I'll clean and oil the bearings."

"I'll do that." Billy spoke up. "Know it inside out, I do, from watching the old man. Lemme do it."

"Thanks, Bobbie, but I've got to get familiar with it myself. You can keep watch through the cracks in the barn wall. Make sure none of those Weltys come sneaking down on us."

"But I'd be better at. . ." Billy laid a hand on the engine, and Susan realised that this broken-down decrepit old carousel was his only contact with his past—with his life. But before she could try to persuade Jim to let Billy do the oiling and cleaning, Jim said firmly, "Looking out's really important. I've got to find out for myself how this thing works, and I can't do that if I'm keeping watch. Okay?"

Susan settled down to draw the drive mechanism, trying to keep the proportions of each part accurate. As she worked she began to realise that Jim was right, that any engine strong enough to turn the gears could rotate the central pole from which hung the whole platform. Give it a strong enough turn and the carousel would come alive again.

She had just finished her second drawing when Billy hissed, "Someun's coming."

Jim leapt from the platform and put his eye to a crack in the wall. "It's George Welty. Any chance you could persuade him to be on our side, Sue?"

"Are you kidding? He bugs me to death at school. He's my total enemy. Let's get out."

They slipped out of the barn, closing the door behind them. Keeping the bulk of the barn between them and the Welty property, they climbed through the strands of wire onto Patterson land and lay down in the dry grass among the clicking whirring grasshoppers.

"Ugh, what's these?" Billy jumped up.

Susan pulled him down again. "Hush up. They won't hurt you, honest. They're kinda fun really. When I was little I used to catch them and try and harness them to my Barbie doll's car."

"Did it work?" Jim whispered.

"Nah. They kept jumping in different directions."

"I was thinking, if we got enough grasshoppers, we could maybe start the carousel. . ."

"Oh, you." Susan started giggling.

"He don't mean that, do he?" Billy asked anxiously.

"Course not. Sshh!"

They lay still. "Hey, you Pattersons." George Welty's voice was startlingly near. "I know you're skulking down there somewheres. Might as well go home. You're not trespassing on our land again. My dad says he'll have the law on you."

The grasshoppers whirred and clicked.

"Is he still there?" Jim whispered after a while.

Susan raised her head cautiously. "I can't see him. He must have gone into the barn."

"Wonder what he's doing."

"Hope he's not messing with my carousel."

"Sshh, Billy, keep your voice down."

"He's taking his time," Jim whispered. "Heck, there's a grasshopper down my shirt."

"He's leaving now. He's going back."

"We'll lie low till he's out of sight."

"But suppose he does call the sheriff?"

"He never saw us. He was just bluffing, trying to scare us off."

"He's out of sight now."

Jim stood up and shook the grasshopper out of his shirt. "Let's get on then. We've wasted enough time already."

They climbed back through the fence and ran to the barn. Susan, who was in the lead, stopped suddenly. "Oh, look!"

Shiny in the sun, fastening the hasp of the barn door, was a large new padlock. Susan tugged at it, in some faint hope that it wasn't fastened. "I can't believe the Weltys'd be so mean." Her eyes filled with angry tears.

"We can get in through the wall easy," Billy said. "Just pull apart them boards we was looking through earlier."

"That's illegal. The barn's part Welty property and only part ours. They'd have the sheriff on us, and then Dad'd be really mad." Jim had taken a pocket knife from his jeans and was poking at the lock as he spoke.

"I'm sure jimmying that thing is every bit as illegal." Susan sniffed back her tears. "Oh, what *are* we going to do?"

"We've got to talk seriously to Dad. See if he can knock some sense into the Weltys."

"You won't tell them anything about Billy here, will you?"

"Course not, dummy."

"I can't figure why all this commotion, kids. You two have known about the old carousel since you were toddlers. Why's it suddenly gotten so important? Why now? *This* summer?"

Susan opened her mouth and shut it again. She stared at Jim, who looked blankly back. "Well. . .", she said slowly and stopped.

Billy burst out, "Gotta get back. Fixing the carousel's the only way to—"

"What Bobbie means, Dad," Jim interrupted quickly, "is that we want to rebuild the carousel. Celebrate the fact that it'll be ninety years old in a couple of years. That. . .er. . .that the county can look back as well as forward. . .that our past's important to us as well as the future. Yeah, that's it."

Tom Patterson looked from Jim to Susan to Billy, a puzzled frown on his face. He shook his head slowly. "I dunno what you kids are really up to, but it doesn't make a whole lot of sense to me. It'd cost a bundle to fix that thing, today's prices, and a lot more time than we can spare. Talking of which, I'll be needing you tomorrow, Jim."

"But—"

"Susan can entertain Bobbie, I'm sure, can't she, Bobbie? And stay away from that barn, d'you hear?"

"Won't you *please* talk to Sam Welty, Dad?"

"Stick my neck out for a fool scheme like that? No, thanks."

"So there we are," Susan said hopelessly, at the council of war in Jim's room after supper.

"You promised you'd get me back. You did."

"I know we did, Billy. And we will. Only—"

"It's got to work," Jim interrupted. "The carousel *was* in the city in 1928 when Great-grandfather bought it. Therefore. . ."

"If you say that one more time, Jim Patterson, I'll

scream. It's not helping one bit. Maybe it went back on its own after it left Billy here. Maybe what's here, all broken down and useless, is like a discarded snake skin. Not the *real* carousel at all."

"You mean I ain't never going to get back?"

"I didn't say that. I don't know. Oh, Billy, why don't you forget about the past and stay with us? It's really nice in 1993. You won't be hungry or cold. And there's good stuff like. . .like TV," she finished weakly.

"With all them wars I seen on that TV? Blowing up kids all over the world. And there *is* people starving. I seen them too. And where I come from's *not* the past. It's where I belong. And I'd rather be a bit hungry and even have the cops after me than get blowed up. And what about Johannes? You two keep forgetting about him. He's sick and he's old and he *needs* me. I gotta get back!" Billy gave a watery sniff and bolted out of the room.

"Oh, poor Billy!" Susan jumped off the bed, but Jim caught her hand. "Leave him alone for a bit, Sue. He won't appreciate you seeing him howling. And we've got to think up a plan."

"You've got an idea?" Susan brightened and then flopped back on the bed with a sigh as Jim shook his head.

"I suppose we *could* push aside a couple of those loose boards, like Billy suggested," she said after a while. "Even if it is just a little bit illegal."

Jim shook his head. "Apart from the fact that we'd be damaging property that's half Weltys', it wouldn't work. Just when I'd figured out how to link up with that old motor of Dad's to kick-start the carousel."

Susan sat up with a bounce. "You mean you *can* get it to work? Fabulous!"

"Hold on. We'd have to haul the motor down there

and fix it up in place of the old steam engine. That'd mean dismantling the boiler and getting it out of there. No way we could do all that if we had to sneak through cracks in the barn. We'd *have* to have the door open, so as to back the truck right in and slide the motor down onto the platform."

Susan sighed and then stuck her chin out. "I'm *not* going to give up. Let's go ahead with our planning as if it *were* all right. Here. . ." She stood up and pulled her drawings out of her jeans pocket. "Got a bit crumpled, I'm afraid, when we had to get out of there in a hurry. Think they'll do?"

Jim took her drawings and smoothed them out on his desk. "Yeah, it'll work. See here, the drive belt from Dad's motor'll loop around here. Then it'll rotate the centre pole and the whole platform."

"Fast enough, do you think?"

"That's the catch, isn't it? The motor can certainly handle the job. But whether it can go fast enough to take Billy back where he came from'll depend on the state of the bearings and whether the platform's still hanging true."

"Huh?"

"If there's a wobble it'll lose energy—you know, like those tops we had as kids, remember? A coloured disc with a spindle through the middle. If you twisted the spindle hard enough it'd go so fast it looked like it vanished. But if you didn't hold it straight or if the floor was bumpy, then it'd just wobble and fall over."

"I *see*. So what we have to do is make sure the pole and the platform are straight and true, and then use Dad's motor to give a big enough twirl. . ."

"Yeah. Then with any luck Billy'll go back. And I must say I won't be sorry. He's an interesting little guy, but every time he's around Mom I come out in a sweat worrying what he'll say or do next. You know something, Sue? Mom's going to *kill* you when she finds out what you did."

"Maybe she'll never know."

"Get real! Sooner or later Aunt Marian's going to phone or write, and then they'll know that your Billy isn't Bobbie Stevens. And they're sure going to want to know exactly who they've been giving house room to all through July."

"Okay, I get the picture. Maybe I'll tell them the truth. It'll be a relief after all these stories."

"They'll never believe you."

"Weird, isn't it? Say, Jim, Billy's been on his own long enough. Let's go and talk to him. See if we can cheer him up."

But Billy wasn't on the porch glider, nor was he in the stables talking to Judy, to whom he'd taken a real shine. Nor in any of the sheds, which is where they looked next.

The sky was slowly darkening and Venus shone as bright as an airplane landing-light just above the western horizon, where a thin band of cloud still caught the last ruddy glow of the sun. Below the sky the wheat was silver, moving slightly in the breeze, like a great sheet of water.

"Bobbie!"

"Hey, Bobbie, where are you?"

Behind them the screen door slammed. "What are you two shouting about?"

"Nothing, Mom. Just a game," Jim said quickly.

The screen door closed again. "Oh, dear, another lie!" Susan whispered.

"Better than telling her we've mislaid him and getting her all upset. Darn it, where'd the kid go?"

"To the carousel, Jim! He must have. It's the only

thing that links him to home."

They hurried along the trail that led north, jogging along in the semi-darkness towards the boundary fence, then turning east towards the shadowy hump of the old round barn.

"That's funny. I thought I saw a flash of light."

"I didn't see anything."

They passed under the weatherbeaten wall. "Jim!" Susan clutched her brother's arm. "Look!"

The barn door was open, the new padlock hanging loose from the hasp. From within the barn a light shone.

CHAPTER SEVEN

Susan and Jim froze in the doorway of the barn, blinded by the glare.

"Get that darn light outta my face," Jim shouted.

"Billy, is that you?" Susan asked at the same moment, putting up her hand to shield her eyes from the light.

The light was lowered and, as they blinked, they were able to see a shadowy figure standing by the carousel.

"*George!*"

"Yep."

"What are you doing here?"

"Just curious. I was in the kitchen last evening and I heard you talking to Dad and Grandpa." He chuckled and Susan felt her face get hot. Now he'd *really* have something to tell the kids about in school next month. "Wanted to see what all the commotion was about. The carousel's not much, is it? Not worth fighting over, I'd say." His flashlight beam traced the worn paint, the rotted leathers, the grime and cobwebs overlaying it all. "Anyway, what are you two doing down here. I reckon Dad'd say you were trespassing."

"We weren't aiming to come in. Not exactly. We were looking for B. . .for Bobbie. And then we saw the open door."

"Who's Bobbie?"

"Our cousin. Bobbie Stevens. From New Hampshire," Jim added.

"This him?" The light flashed around the carousel to the far side, where, leaning against the Indian pony, was. . .

"Oh, Billy!" Susan ran around the platform and hugged him. "You scared us to death running off like that. You could have got lost."

"I'm lost right now, ain't I?" He turned a tear-smeared face to her and then buried it again in the pony's wooden neck.

George Welty turned his flashlight onto Jim. "You know, that's the second time Susan's called him 'Billy'. I thought you said his name was Bobbie Stevens."

"It is. He is."

"From New Hampshire?"

"Yeah."

"He sure doesn't have a New England accent, does he?"

"Uh. . ." Jim hesitated and then went on crossly. "For pete's sake take that light outta my eyes, kid. This isn't an interrogation."

"Maybe it is." George sat on the edge of the platform and put the flashlight down beside him, so that its light ran between the triple circle of carved legs, casting bars of light and shadow across the barn. "Why don't you tell me what's really going on?"

"Why the heck should I?"

"Maybe because I'm the one that's got the key of the padlock to this here barn door."

Jim sat down beside him and stared. "Are you saying you're on our side?"

"Maybe."

"Why d'you want to stick your neck out?"

George grinned and rubbed his freckled nose with the back of his hand. "It's kinda because of what Susan was saying last evening. It's crazy to have a feud going on when we could be friends. And partly I'm just plain curious. My granddad asked Susan here why she was so all-fired eager to get the old carousel going *now*. Why not last year? Why not next? Why ever?"

"What did she tell him?" Jim asked cautiously.

"Some garbage about anniversaries. I mean it was obvious she was winging it, and I'm kinda curious to find out the *real* reason."

Jim hesitated.

"Hey, if you don't want to tell me, that's just fine. You can leave now and I'll lock the door. No harm done and no hard feelings."

Jim rubbed his hair up the wrong way. "The problem is, George, you wouldn't believe me if I *did* tell you."

"Try me. It's something to do with him, isn't it?" He jerked his thumb to where Billy still leant against the Indian pony, Susan's arm around his shoulders. "That guy who's name should be Bobbie, only sometimes it's Billy, when Susan isn't thinking. The one who doesn't come from New Hampshire. Hey, is he a runaway from reform school, something like that? Have you guys been hiding him out in the barn? Is that's what it's all about?"

"Well. . ."

"But why would you go to all this trouble about starting up the carousel? That's a fancy cover-up, isn't it?"

"He's not a runaway. At least, not exactly. He's. . .well, he's not from *here*."

"Well, I know *that*."

"I mean, he's not from 1993."

"Right!"

"It's the honest truth, George. And you must swear not to tell a living soul, okay?"

George chuckled. "Go on. It sounds good so far."

"I tell you it's the truth. I'm not kidding you. This carousel's kind of like a time machine. Under the right conditions, if you go fast enough, it spins the rider off into the future."

"You've got to be. . ." George shone the flashlight in Jim's face again. "Gee, you're not kidding, are you? Wow!" He looked around at the grimy animals. "You mean, if we could get this old thing going again, we could go into the future and see everything? Man, that'd be fantastic! We could—"

"No." Jim broke into his excited chatter. "It's not like that. You don't understand. This is like the terminal. The end of the line. As far as the carousel's concerned this *is* the future."

George stared at Jim. His mouth slowly fell open. "Wait a minute." He turned his flashlight towards the Indian pony again. "What you're saying is this kid, this Billy-Bobbie, is outta the *past?*"

Jim nodded. "You've got it. Susan found him down here, and she pretended he was our cousin Bobbie, so he could sleep in a proper bed and get decent meals."

George nodded. "Smart move, but tricky. He doesn't *look* like he's a cousin of yours. And he sure doesn't sound like he comes from New England."

"Tell me about it!" Jim gave a bitter laugh. "It's been murder trying to keep him out of Mom's way. I'm sure she suspects something, but she doesn't know quite what to do about it. The real problem is we've got to get him back where he came from before the next full moon—or before Mom discovers for sure he isn't Bobbie Stevens, whichever happens first."

"You mean you really *are* aiming to restore this old wreck? In less than a month? You've got to be kidding!"

"No, of course we can't do all that. We've just got to get the drive mechanism working again. Make sure the platform's clear and sitting true. Then we aim to send the carousel and Billy right back into the past again."

"That old boiler's never going to work, I bet you."

"I know. We were in the middle of testing it yesterday when your dad came and threw us out. It leaks like a sieve."

George's face got red. "I'm sorry about Dad. And about. . ." He stopped and his face got even redder. "Look. When I came down this morning and put the padlock on the door, you guys *were* out there, hiding in the grass, weren't you?"

"Yep."

"And I guess you heard everything I said. I was just sounding off, you know. It didn't mean anything."

"It's okay, George. Forget it."

"Friends then?" George held out his hand.

Jim took it. "Friends. So we can count on you to let us in here? Maybe lend us one of the keys?"

"Sure you can have a key. But I'm not just walking

away from this. I'm going to help you get this thing
going. I wouldn't miss it for anything in the world. A
time machine." He slapped the platform. "And I'm sitting on it!"

Susan turned from comforting Billy. "You *told*
him?" She glared at Jim. "How *could* you?" What's
school going to be like next year, she thought, with
George Welty kidding her about time machines in
front of all the guys? A Zeke's Folly rerun.

"Hold on, Sue. He's on our side."

"He's a Welty," she snapped.

"Look, Sue," George interrupted. "We're friends
now. Jim and I shook hands on it. I only—"

"Don't call me Sue. You're not family. And who says
you and I are friends? I never shook hands with you."
She tried to stare him down, chin in the air, remembering how George had tied her braids to the back of
her chair in Grade One, and how he'd hidden a toad in
her desk in Grade Two. How he'd smeared her scrib-
bler with crazy glue in Grade Three, so it had stuck to
the shelf under her desk and she'd just about gone
nuts trying to pick it up. All the way up through Grade
Six he'd thought up rotten tricks to play on her. Not
on the other kids. Just *her*. Picking on *her*.

Except this last year. Funny. He hadn't teased her
once all year. She wondered why and found herself
blushing. That made her madder than ever. "Why, I
wouldn't be friends with you if you were the last—"

"Susan, hush up and listen," Jim yelled. "He's going
to help us get Billy back home."

"He *is*?" She turned to George. "You're not going to
tell your dad? You're going to let us in the barn?"

"Sure. Like I said, we're friends. Leastways Jim and
I are. And last night you were the one talking about
ending the feud. Didn't you mean it?"

"I guess." She felt suddenly ashamed. Here she was, thinking about herself again when poor Billy was trapped in the wrong end of the twentieth century.

"Wanna shake on it?"

Shamefacedly Susan held out her hand. She glanced quickly at his smiling freckled face and then away again. She felt all mixed up, kind of happy, but kind of regretful for the loss of the enemy she'd had all these years. What'd it be like having George as an ally?

She turned away to where Billy still stood apart from them, clinging to the neck of his favourite pony as if it was his only link to the past. Which it is, she realised, and had a sudden glimpse of herself way off in the future, when she'd be very old, coming back to this house, this barn. Seeing them again. Would they be run-down or completely gone, replaced with something totally different, like a shopping mall? How weird it would be. But at least growing old into one's own future was natural. But to be pushed into the future before one had had a chance to live one's growing up, one's adult life, that must be totally terrifying.

"Hey, Billy, it's okay. George is going to help us fix the carousel. We'll get you back. You mustn't give up."

He turned a grubby tear-stained face to her. "No kidding?"

"No kidding. We'd better go back to the house before Mom starts worrying. Let's clean you up a bit first." She fished in her jeans pocket for a tissue. "Here. Spit on this." She scrubbed at his face and then looked at him doubtfully. "We'd better sneak you into the house and under a shower, or Mom'll think we've been beating up on you or something."

"Go ahead with him, Sue. I'll fill George in on our plans."

It's not fair, Susan thought. *Jim's leaving me out again. I found Billy. I looked after him. I was the one had the idea of pretending he was cousin Bobbie. It was me promised to get the carousel going. It was even me went into the Welty lion's den. So now I'm being sidelined, while Jim's telling George all his plans.*

She wrestled with her jealousy as she persuaded Billy to have a shower and go to bed and not worry. She told herself that the only thing that really mattered was getting Billy back into his own place and time, and that who helped him get there wasn't important.

Next morning, she was able to ask Jim, with only the smallest twinge of jealousy, what he and George had planned the night before.

"He thinks my idea of using the portable diesel motor's great. Only problem is we'll be combining next week. No way I can get out of that. Guess working on the carousel will be up to you and Billy and George."

"Okay," she said meekly. "We'll work on cleaning and oiling everything, so when you *are* free we can attach the motor to the drive and be ready to go."

Mid July was hot and dry. The sun blazed down and the chopped straw from the combiner rose in a fine golden haze over the land. Everyone got up extra early to take advantage of every moment of daylight, and Susan had to do all the necessary chores that Dad and Jim usually did between them.

Most days she and Billy found George already working when they got down to the barn. They cleaned every last bit of rubbish from under the platform and Billy showed them how to tighten the arms that radiated out from the central pole like the spokes of an umbrella, and the rods that joined them to the platform, so it hung free and clear from the centre pole.

The barn was like an oven long before noon and it held the heat overnight, so every day seemed warmer. They decided they wouldn't risk leaving the door open, in case it attracted the attention of anyone passing by on the road, people like the Weltys, who weren't busy harvesting, since they raised cattle instead of wheat and rye.

"Though we'll be taking off another hay crop pretty soon," George said. "It's been a real good year. I'll have to help Dad out then. Already he's beginning to ask where I spend my days."

"What'd you tell him?"

"Just that I've been checking fences a lot lately."

"We could never have managed so far without you. Thanks."

"Why, you're welcome. Hey, you look cute with grease on your face."

"Thanks. I guess." Susan blushed and scrubbed her cheek.

Finally the combining was done and Jim was able to escape down to the barn. With the four of them working together they tested the suspension of the carousel, all of them pushing at the great wooden platform. "Come on. Just a bit harder."

"I'm busting myself now."

"Come on. We can do it."

At last they overcame the inertia and the platform squeaked, trembled and moved an inch. Then

another. "Don't stop now!" Jim yelled. "Not now we've
got some momentum."

Like a creature waking from a long sleep the
carousel began to turn.

"Okay. We can stop now. It must be straight and
level and those bearings working right or we'd never
have budged it. Great! Now all we've got to do is to
put the motor in the middle and connect it to the
drive system. Wait for the full moon, Bobbie, and you
should be on your way."

"You mean it? It's really gonna work?" Billy's face
shone and Susan felt a sudden twinge of panic.
They'd promised him so much. Suppose they
couldn't deliver? It was like running down a steep
hill; okay so long as you didn't let yourself think
about where you were going to put each foot.
Because once you started thinking about it instead of
trusting your body, then over you'd go. The momentum of fixing the carousel was like running downhill.
But what now?

Billy was staring at her, his eyes narrow, his mouth
tight. She had a sudden flash of the urchin who had
had to steal bread to survive. Why in the world would
he want to go back to *that*?

"It's gonna work?" Billy insisted.

"Sure it is. Jim's a whiz with engines, aren't you,
Jim?"

"Just so long as it doesn't fly apart at that speed,"
Jim said absently. He'd been talking to George, pay-
ing no attention to Billy's need for reassurance. Susan
could have killed him for that casual remark, but
Billy wasn't bothered. "She'll hold together." He patted the platform affectionately.

"Four days till full moon. Can we do it in time?"

"Hauling the motor down here and bolting it to the

floor's the only chore. George and I can handle it easy, can't we?"

"No problem. Time to go, I guess." He solemnly snapped the padlock shut as they left. "Got to keep those varmint Pattersons out. You've got your key, Jim?"

"Right here in my pocket, George."

His eyes twinkle when he's joking, Susan thought. *I never noticed that before. And those freckles are kind of neat. School in another month. It'll be fun, though. I guess I'm really looking forward to it.*

"Come on, you two. I'll race you up to the house." She set off with a spurt of sudden happiness, but it was really too hot for running, and she'd slowed down by the time she reached the yard. Mom had been doing a massive wash, and every quilt was hanging out, brightly waving in the breeze, so the house looked like a ship decorated for the Fourth of July. Mom was outside, feeling if they were dry enough to fold and bring in.

Susan waved and went on into the house, where the phone was ringing desperately as if it had been ringing for a long time. Why in the world didn't Grandpa answer it? She picked up the receiver.

"Hello?"

"Susan, it's Aunt Marian. How are you, dear?"

"Just. . .just fine, thanks." Susan sat down abruptly as her knees gave way.

"Is your mother in?"

"No. No, I'm sorry but she's out right now." Susan looked out the kitchen window to where Mom was folding quilts into a laundry basket. Well, it *was* strictly true. "Can I take a message?"

"Yes, please. I've only got a moment. We've been visiting friends on the west coast. With only a bit of a detour we can drop in on you. Two or three days from now, if all goes well. I'll phone Veronica later, but do tell her our plans, won't you, dear? Wouldn't want to invade you with our bunch without due warning." A laugh at the end of the phone. Susan stared at it wordlessly. "Susan, dear, are you there?"

"Yes. Sure, Aunt Marian, I got the message."

"Sure you're all right, child? You're certainly silent."

"Fine." Susan tried to pull herself together. "We'll really look forward to seeing you. And the kids."

"Tell Jim that Bobbie's determined to beat him at checkers this time. He's been working on it. Oh-oh. There's the car horn. Got to go. 'Bye, dear."

Susan put the phone down and sat staring numbly at the vinyl floor until Mom's voice interrupted her thoughts. "Give us a hand, dear."

She jumped. Mom was waiting at the screen door, the basket piled up to her chin with folded quilts. Susan held open the door for her and then slipped through.

"Excuse me, Mom. Got to talk to the others."

"Was that the phone I heard a while back? Did you catch it?"

But Susan was gone, running to the barn where Billy was giving Judy her evening feed under the supervision of Jim. Jim took the news with a shrug. "It was bound to happen. Lucky you got away with it so long, Sue."

"*I* got away with it?"

"It was your bright idea."

"But what'll we do *now*?"

"Get Billy back where he belongs before they get here and ruin it all. Then you'll just have to 'fess up."

"Mom's going to be *furious*. What in the world'll we tell her about Billy?"

"As little as possible, I guess."

At the sound of his name Billy turned from stroking Judy's neck. "You're going to get me back okay?"

"You bet. Maybe sooner than we planned, that's all."

"What about the full moon?"

"We don't *know* that it's really important. Not exactly anyway. We're going to have to try and send you off the night after next, before Aunt Marian and the gang arrive. If it doesn't work, well, you'll just have to hide out in the barn again, and we'll try on the night of the full moon." Jim's calm voice had the desired effect, and Billy looked less worried.

That night, though, Jim slipped into her room. "What worries me, Sue," he said abruptly, parking himself on the end of her bed, "is running the carousel at full speed *before* the full moon."

"Why? We'll just run it again later if it doesn't work."

"I've been thinking about that. We may only have the one chance. At that speed the whole thing could fly apart. I mean, it's just been sitting there for over sixty years."

Susan stared, her mouth open. When she'd taken it in she shook her head. "We simply mustn't risk it then. We've got to wait till the night of the full moon."

"But how'll we hide Billy that long? Once Mom and Dad know about him, they're bound to wonder who he is, get the sheriff looking for him. The barn won't be safe enough."

Susan hugged her knees. "So we risk losing the carousel if an attempt *before* the full moon doesn't work. Or we risk Billy getting arrested if we wait. How on earth can we decide what's best?"

"Wait and see. Tomorrow we'll haul the motor down to the barn and get it all set up. Once that's done we can start worrying about the timing." Jim walked over to the door. As he opened it there was a scuffle on the other side. "Hey, young Bobbie, what are you doing out there?"

"Nothin'."

"Off to bed with you then." He closed the door again.

"D'you suppose he heard us?" Susan whispered.

Jim shrugged. "He'll have to know the odds sooner or later. Don't lose any sleep over it."

Thanks a lot, big brother, Susan grumbled to herself after he'd left. Moonlight filled the room and the moving drapes sent patterns of light and shade across the floor. Would the platform fly apart at the first try? Could they get Billy back? And if they couldn't, what in the world were they to do? Mom would never let him stay on, an unknown boy with no tellable history. It was bad enough worrying about what in the world Mom would say when she found out he wasn't Bobbie, that Susan had made up the whole thing. But the truth was so completely unbelievable.

It had all been such a great adventure in the beginning. Then one little lie, just to help Billy, had led to another. To a whole mountain of lies. *What a mess I've got us into.* She groaned and punched her pillow, turning it over, and then over again, hunting for sleep.

The motor Jim had in mind was stored in one of the sheds, a small heavy all-purpose "donkey" that could be used for any number of chores around the place. They waited until Dad had left for the south section and then levered it up onto a ramp and so onto the tailgate of the truck.

"I think my arms are going to fall off," Susan gasped.

"Cheer up. It'll be easier at the other end, with gravity working for us. And George'll be there to help. It'll be a snap." Jim was as optimistic as ever. Obviously *he* hadn't lost any sleep the night before.

It wasn't a snap. It took them a long tense hour to shift the dead weight across the platform to the centre without destroying any of the animals on the way. It took them another hour to get it into the right position, and another to drill holes in the concrete so that they could bolt it to the floor. But at last it was done and they collapsed onto the platform.

All except for Billy. "Aren't you going to hook it up now?" His eyes blazed with excitement.

"Give us a break, fella," Jim groaned. "First I've got to see if the drive belt's the right length. If not—"

"Might be something over at our place," George interrupted.

In the end it was late afternoon before Jim and George had the motor hooked up to the drive mechanism that turned the big cog at the bottom of the centre pole.

"Start it up," Billy begged, his voice trembling.

George carefully poured in the fuel. Jim adjusted the starter and pressed the button. The tough little donkey coughed out black smoke and then chugged away. Jim engaged the drive mechanism. The belt tightened and took hold.

"Steady does it," George whispered.

"Okay. I've got it." Jim's hand moved the control lever forward. The engine changed its tune from a race to a steady thrum. The cog wheel moved. The centre pole turned, carrying with it the outstretched arms, like the spokes of an umbrella, from which hung the vertical poles that held up the platform. Slowly, creakily, the platform began to turn. The giraffe, which had stared at the barn door for over sixty years, turned its head north and then west. The armoured leader, the Indian pony, the sea monster and the chariot slowly followed.

It was magic, like the people in the Sleeping Beauty story waking up after their hundred years' sleep, thought Susan, and shivers prickled up her arms. Dusty, worn and decayed though they were, the animals seemed suddenly alive.

Jim released the clutch and the carousel slowly glided to a stop. He turned off the engine. Grinning from ear to ear, he and George pounded each other on the back. "We've done it! We've done it!"

"Why d'you stop?" Billy pulled at their arms, prying them apart. "Why don't you go on?"

"Hold on, fella. Don't be in such a hurry. We'll try it tomorrow night, before Aunt Marian and the kids turn up. That's only one night away from the full moon."

"But. . ."

"Time for supper anyway." George glanced at his watch. "I'm off before I have to answer too many questions. See you tomorrow. Goodnight, Susan."

"G'night." Susan answered him automatically. She rubbed her arms and shivered in spite of the heat. The carousel *was* magic. For the first time she really believed that it had the power to take Billy back in time. Up till now, she realised, it had all been words, promises, whatever Billy wanted to hear. But now. . .

The weird dreamlike feeling clung to her all evening. A kind of floating, like you felt before coming down with the flu. She managed to avoid a game of cribbage with Grandpa and went to bed early. Billy had been more than usually quiet all evening, and jumped up as she said goodnight to the family, as if he, too, was glad to get away.

"Goodnight, Bobbie," she said to him in the passage, remembering, with a sense of panic, as she used his pretend name, that Aunt Marian and the real Bobbie would be here in two days. "See you in the morning," she said brightly, hoping he didn't catch her fear.

He stopped at the door of Jim's room and looked at her, as if what she'd said had a special significance. "Look, Miss—I mean, Susan. Thanks for everything you done for me. I ain't never going to forget it."

"That's all right." She smiled vaguely and, still wrapped in the strange feeling, undressed automatically, showered and fell into bed.

She woke all at once and completely, as if it were morning, to find the moon shining on her face. Billy's last words echoed in her memory. "Thanks for everything you done for me. I ain't never going to forget it." Almost as if he were saying goodbye.

She sat up abruptly and looked at her bedside clock. Just twelve-fifteen. The house was as still as if it were holding its breath. Only the solemn ticktock of the clock in the hall broke the silence.

She slipped out of bed, eased open her door and padded in bare feet down the hall to Jim's room. She turned the handle, careful not to let it spring back, and peered inside. The moon didn't shine into the windows on this side of the house, but she could clearly see the white oblong of Billy's bed, the sheet thrown back.

Silently Susan left and, back in her own room, scrambled into jeans, sweater and socks. Flashlight in hand, she slipped out of the house. Faster on Judy, she thought, and made for the stable. The horses stirred, stamped their feet and nickered sleepily as she shone the light on them. Quickly she slipped bridle and bit on Judy and led her out. It had been ages since she'd ridden bareback, but she'd save a few precious moments by not taking the time to saddle her up.

Judy picked her way along the path, shying skittishly at moon shadows as if she'd never seen them before. "Come on, old girl. Get moving!" She dug her heels in Judy's fat sides and clicked her tongue encouragingly.

She could smell diesel fuel before they had even reached the barn. She slid down Judy's side and hitched her to the fence. How'd Billy get into the barn? she asked herself as she ran around to the door. Then she remembered that Jim had the key in his jeans pocket. Billy sure didn't miss a trick.

The door was ajar and she could hear the cheerful chug of the engine and, above it, almost inaudible, a whisper, like the wind through wheat before a storm. "Stop, Billy! Don't!"

But she was too late. The animals spun by, faster and faster. She caught a glimpse of Billy, astride the Indian pony, close enough so that for one millionth of a second she could have reached out and touched him. But by the time her brain had registered his nearness he was gone.

Now the animals were spinning by so fast she could hardly see them. Like that top I had as a kid, she thought. All the colours of the rainbow, but when it spun true and fast they turned to a white blur. It was like that now. The carousel was a huge top. She took a step forward, but something pushed her back. Like a wind. But different. More like electricity. She could feel the skin on her arms prickle, the hair on her head stir and lift. Like the time when she'd been caught in a summer storm and a lightning bolt had struck a fence post close to where she'd been standing.

She backed into the doorway, clutching the frame, afraid that she'd be sucked into the power, sucked back into the past. Now the carousel was vanishing in a milky haze, a shimmer. Or was it just the moonlight dazzling her eyes?

She blinked and now she could see the animals again, the giraffe chasing the lion, chasing the pony. Round and round. Slower and slower. The engine coughed. The platform shuddered to a stop.

Susan walked slowly forward. "Billy?" Her voice echoed in the emptiness of the barn. A rat scuffled in the darkness under the platform. A patch of dark in the moonlight caught her eye. Billy's pajamas, the Star Trek ones that had once been hers. She moved her flashlight around. The grimy long johns, which she'd hung on a nail on the barn wall twenty-six days ago, were gone.

Billy had left as he had come, taking with him only what he'd brought. Susan stroked the neck of the Indian pony. Had he made it safely back to the time and place he had left? Would he be reunited with the old man, Johannes? She would never know. It was like reading a book the last pages of which had been torn out.

She shivered and walked slowly out of the barn, leaving the door open, so that the moon shone in on the sleeping carousel.

CHAPTER EIGHT: 1908

As Billy clung to the worn neck of the Indian pony, he felt the platform begin to turn beneath him, felt his pony carried forward and around. Faster and faster, like he was riding across the great plains, till the wind lifted his hair, till it streamed across his face and he had to press his cheek against the pony's grimy wooden neck. The barn seemed to disappear and he saw the moonlit milkiness again. The blinding shimmer. He shut his eyes and clung to the pony.

Before he had even opened them again he could feel the sleek fresh paint against his cheek. His hands fumbled for and found the reins, new leather cleaned just the day before. Was he home? He was almost afraid to look.

Paint gleamed in the moonlight. Eyes shone. The brass fittings were like pale gold, and the horsetails stood out frisky and fresh. Giraffe and lion, tiger and sea monster. As Billy slid to the platform his knees buckled under him and he had to lean against the pony, his arm around its neck. Around him the park slept. The gravel pathways radiated out from the carousel, alternate bands of moonshine and shadow. The trees and bushes were like dark sentinels on guard. At the end of one path stood the little hut.

He ran on bare silent feet, not caring for the sharp gravel. The door was ajar, just as he had left it, the moonlight a white stripe across the floor. The old man lay on his back, the blanket up to his armpits, his arms tucked neatly along each side of his body. He was very still. Billy's heart lurched in his chest and he clutched the doorpost. Then Johannes's eyes opened.

"Billy boy!" he said and then began to sing in a high reedy voice, "Where have you been all the day, my Billy boy?" His voice broke and he began to cough.

Billy sat on the side of the bed and held out a mug of water. "Oh, you'll never believe it. Not in a million years."

The old man struggled up on one elbow and peered at him. "What have you been up to then? Why, you've been riding the carousel, that's it, ain't it?"

Billy nodded. "But I think it's broke. I went too fast. Too far. Nearly didn't get back." He told Johannes the whole story. "I'm sorry if it's broke," he finished. "I shouldn't have done it."

The old man was silent for a while. Then he shifted with a grunt. "P'raps it's as well. If it had spun me that far into the future, I doubt anybody'd raise a finger to help me back, like those youngsters did for you. Not a useless old man like me."

"You *ain't* useless! But oh, Johannes, you'd be that

put out to see what the carousel looks like in the future. Mucky and broken down. Ain't been used in years and years. Them kids were talking about putting it to rights, though. Getting it going again."

"Maybe they will, Billy boy."

"Maybe. They were keen enough all right, but not much gumption. They didn't know. . . Wish I coulda. . ." He stopped, feeling the colour rise in his cheeks, and reached across to straighten the old man's blanket.

Johannes gave him a long steady look. "Kinda hankering to stay, were you? Why didn't you then?"

"No. Never. Wasn't my place. There weren't nobody belonging to me there."

"You came back because of me, didn't you?" Johannes's voice was husky. "I'd never have expected that. In fact. . ." He paused and gave Billy another of his long straight looks. "In fact, I thought you'd have run off, once you knew where I stashed my savings. Sorry, son."

It was the first time Johannes had ever called him "son". Billy swallowed and was silent. Then he spoke slowly. "Look, I near did run off when you give me the money for that 'medicine'. But I didn't. Nor I won't neither. You done a whole lot for me. We're partners, if that's all right with you."

"I reckon we are then. So long as you don't regret coming back."

Billy shook his head. "Never, only 'cept for helping them kids fix the carousel. They don't know nothing about the tails and the leathers and getting the colours right and all."

"So you'd like to go into the future just to show them what our carousel is supposed to look like?"

"That's it. The rest, they can keep it. Funny world, I

thought. Something called pollution. And a bomb. Nope. This here's where I belong."

Johannes was deep in thought. "You'd be pretty near a hundred by the time they get around to restoring the carousel, I reckon," he said at last.

"Meaning?"

"Meaning that's the only time travel you've got available. Day by day till you get to where they're at."

"More likely I'll be pushing up the daisies by then."

"There's always your children. Or your grandchildren."

"How d'you mean?"

"We could write it out, the two of us. A catalogue of the animals and their proper colours and the harnesses and tails."

"And the pretty paintings on them boards in the middle what hide the drive. . ."

"The rounding boards. How many times've I told you their name already? Yep, I reckon between the two of us we could do that. Put it all in a book. Drawings and descriptions."

"What then? How do we get it into the future?"

"You don't. You hang onto it till you've got kids of your own. Hand it on to them. Tell them the first one's got a kid has to give the book to them. Then *his* child, or *hers* as it might be, is to take the book down to the place where the carousel's at. Late August, 1993, so there's no chance of them meeting you as a boy."

Billy chuckled. "My great-grandson, that'd be, wouldn't it?" He counted on his fingers. "Kind of time travel."

"Reckon so."

"Safest kind."

Billy sat on the edge of Johannes's bed and looked

at the old man. He was really better now, you could tell that. The hectic flush in his cheeks had faded and his blue eyes were clear again. Only his twisted back and his knotted hands gave away his age. Not much different from old Luke Patterson. Susan had boasted a lot about the great medicines they'd got in the future, but it seemed that old bones were still old bones.

"I learned a game there," he remembered, thinking of Susan's grandpa. "Called cribbage. I'll teach you if you like."

The old man's eyes twinkled. "I look forward to it, son."

Billy reached forward to straighten the old man's pillow and his nose twitched. "Tomorrow you and me are going to the baths. You're pretty ripe, old man."

" 'Tain't Saturday yet."

"In the future they wash all over every day. In a 'shower'. Sometimes twice a day."

"Let's not get carried away, Billy boy. You'll have me rusted out and in my grave before I'm ready." He clutched the blanket to his throat in mock fear.

Billy laughed. He laughed until the tears came to his eyes and wouldn't stop. He wiped his face on the sleeve of his long johns. "Old man, how'd we ever get on without each other?"

CHAPTER NINE: 1995

The great day had finally come. July the Fourth, 1995. The round barn was decorated with flags and red, white and blue bunting. Just about everyone in the whole county was there. The town band was lined up under the platform where the mayor and the head of the chamber of commerce sat, along with the Patterson family. They waited for the Weltys to arrive. There was their van now, easing through the crowd.

"Gee, I hope nothing goes wrong *this* time," Susan whispered to George after he'd wheeled his grandfather's chair up onto the platform and got him settled.

"Don't worry. Granddad's promised to be good."

Then the speeches began, while the hot sun shone down on the crowd. Susan's attention drifted away, to that other day, two summers ago. Right through the August after Billy'd gone they'd worked on restoring the animals. Susan had insisted. Working helped fill in the gap that his going had left. But they knew so little. Should they make the animals pretty, or somehow find out exactly how they *should* look? It was while they'd been arguing over this that the red convertible had pulled up by the barn.

"Hi, there. I'm looking for Pattersons."

"You've found them. Some of us anyway. I'm Jim Patterson. This is my sister Sue."

"Well, that's a relief!" The young woman got out of the car. She was in her mid twenties, with short dark hair. "My name's Anne Taylor."

They shook hands and Jim introduced George.

"George *Welty*?"

They stared. "How'd you know?" Susan asked. "Have you been out this way before? Have we ever met? I can't recollect. . ."

"No. I've never been in eastern Colorado before. But. . ." The stranger hesitated and Susan saw a blush darkening the freckled cheekbones. "This sounds really weird, I know, but I was told to come out here and find the place where the Patterson and Welty spreads meet. I was told there'd be a barn. And a carousel. There *is* a carousel in there, isn't there? Then I was to introduce myself to Susan, Jim and George as a relative of 'Billy's'. Does that make any sense?"

Susan had screamed out loud. Remembering that day, she could still feel the sudden happiness and relief. "*Billy!* So he got back safely?"

"Excuse me?"

"How is he?" Jim interrupted. "Oh, I suppose by now he's. . ."

"My great-grandfather died peacefully in August last year. He was ninety-six. A good age. What *do* you mean: 'he got back safely'?"

They looked at each other. "Well, it's kind of hard to explain," Susan said slowly. "I don't know. . ."

"Never mind. It's just—well, I can't figure it out. How he *knew* you'd be here. How you seem to know him. Nobody calls him 'Billy'; he's been Grandpa or Great-grandpa for as long as I can remember. And his travelling days are long over."

They couldn't help smiling at that, secret glances towards each other. Anne Taylor flushed at their smiles, and Susan pulled herself together. "I'm sorry. Won't you come up to the house? Stay for lunch?"

"That's very kind, but I can't stay."

"Have you come far?"

"From the coast. Just north of San Francisco. I'm only here to give you this sketchbook."

She reached into the car and brought out a large linenbound book. Jim took it and opened it at random. "It's the carousel!" George and Susan crowded round to look over his shoulder. "Billy did these?"

"He and an old friend, a man who used to work for the Philadelphia Toboggan Company."

"Johannes!" Susan exclaimed. "So he did get better."

Jim kicked her on the shin and she bit her lip. "Sorry. Not thinking."

Anne Taylor smiled a slightly strained smile. "You seem to know more about my family history than I do," she said lightly.

"These are beautiful." George changed the subject, turning over the pages carefully. "Look at the detail!"

"There's something in the beginning. Some kind of dedication," Anne Taylor pointed out.

Jim read it out loud. "For Susan, Jim and George. So the carousel may run again—but not too fast. Billy boy."

Anne Taylor laughed awkwardly. "It never made any sense to my dad or me. Some private joke. Susan. Jim. George." She looked slowly from one to the other, and her face was pale. She put on her sunglasses. "What a coincidence," she said uncertainly. "That dedication was written eighty-five years ago."

After that she got quickly back into her red convertible and drove out of their lives, leaving the linenbound book with its brown edges and the perfect paintings of the fifteen menagerie animals of the outer circle and the decorations on the centre boards.

Susan touched the dedication page. "It makes him seem so close."

"Now I *really* believe that we can get this thing restored. With *this*."

"Zeke's Folly."

"Billy boy's. . ."

In the weeks after Anne Taylor had left Susan felt suddenly light. It was as if a cloud hanging over her had vanished. A cloud of worrying whether Billy had got safely back, or if he'd been marooned in some other time, unable to go home. Knowing he was okay made it easier to bear the memory of the anger of Mom and Dad, when she'd confessed, the morning after Billy had vanished, that he wasn't cousin Bobbie, but a total stranger she had found in the old barn.

"I knew there was something odd about the boy!" Dad had said.

"He could have been an escaped criminal. We could all have been murdered in our beds." Mom's reply was predictable. Then she'd turned to Dad. "What d'you mean, *you* knew there was something odd about him? I remember telling you that first night that he wasn't like any child of Marian's, but you wouldn't listen. Told me not to fuss!"

Unfortunately, this distraction hadn't lasted long and they'd both turned on Susan. The awful thing was having no excuse for lying and deceiving. All she could say was, "I was sorry for him. He was hungry and alone."

"Why didn't you tell us? We'd have got in touch with the Children's Aid. I just can't believe it of you!"

And so it had gone on, and it seemed, for months, that her naughtiness was never going to be forgotten. But eventually it was, and she could bear it because of knowing that Billy had got back. That he wasn't trapped in some other place and time, perhaps with nobody to help him.

Everything had turned out all right. And they had the directions to make this the most perfect carousel in the world.

So here they were, two years after Billy had come and gone. Dad and Sam Welty slowly brought the speech-making to an end and declared the carousel open. The lineup for rides was already forming, but the first ride had to be formal, like the married couple dancing alone at the wedding reception.

"So who's going to ride the leader this time?" Irving Welty stuck his skinny neck out, just like a tortoise, Susan thought. She looked at Grandpa. *Oh, don't let it start all over again*, she begged silently. There was a long electric silence, while the two old men stared each other down.

Then George broke the deadlock by jumping from the platform and holding his hand up to Susan. "We are," he said firmly.

Together they climbed on the back of the armoured leader. Jim crossed the platform to the centre and started up the engine. The band struck up "In the

Good Old Summertime", and the platform began to turn.

Perched on the horse, her arms clasped around George's waist, Susan laughed. It's over now, the feud between the Pattersons and the Weltys. Publicly dissolved in front of the whole county, as it had been blown up nearly seventy years before.

The carousel slowed and stopped. Susan slipped off the leader and claimed the brown pony in the outer circle. She slipped her feet in the stirrups and took up the fresh new reins. The platform began to turn again. She felt the earth turn under her, felt it trace its circle around the sun. Felt the whole solar system wind around the spinning galaxy in the biggest circle of all. From a day to a year. A year to two hundred and thirty million years.

Backwards from Anne Taylor in her red convertible, back to Billy boy, barefoot in the city streets. Forward. . .where to? Life *is* time travel, she thought, her spare hand caressing the fullblown rose that hung from the harness of the Indian pony. Tomorrow and the next day and the next. I can't wait for all the exciting things that are going to happen to me!

The carousel turned round and round.

Acknowledgements

The story of *Where Have You Been, Billy Boy?* was inspired by the carousel PTC #8, which was originally installed in the Elitch Gardens, Denver, in 1905. Now, beautifully and authentically restored, its carved animals turn to the tune of a Wurlitzer Monster Military Band Organ on the Kit Carson County Fairgrounds, Burlington, Colorado.

Many thanks to Mary Fritsch, Ridgewood, New Jersey, of the American Carousel Association; to Marianne Stevens, Roswell, New Mexico; and Sue Hegarty of the American Carousel Museum in San Francisco, all of whom answered my questions and steered me in the direction of many beautiful books on the art of the carousel.